A Study in Silver

Rhiannon D. Elton

Dedicated to Nikki
*Some days when it's hard to write, I keep going because
I know I have to finish the story so you can read the
ending.*

Get More of the Magic & Mystery…

subscribe.rhiannoneltonauthor.com/more

If you want more clues, more magic and more mystery, let me know by going to the Case of the Bitter Draught subscribe page.

You'll get clues, maps, sketches, behind the scenes stories, lore and much more! You'll also be the first to know when a new story is coming out so you can solve the mystery before your friends.

If you sign up with the magical link below, you'll also get a free downloadable map to follow Wolflock's journey to Mystentine University.

subscribe.rhiannoneltonauthor.com/more

Declaration of Intention

Merry meet,

The purpose of the books the author writes is to give representation to as many peoples, creatures and landscapes as they can. Although written from the perspective of a Caucasian teenage boy, the author hopes to offer a light into the harmony of different cultures and creeds of people. The author's aim is to promote harmony, understanding and compassion in all areas, while also inspiring readers to stand up against injustice and be critical thinkers in life.

While the author does their best to research, interview and highlight the best parts of people, they are only human and can make mistakes. The author asks you gently educate them by sending them an email in order to discuss anything that may have caused harm to a group of people unintentionally.

The author believes that the cure for ignorance is education, but please approach the topic cordially in order to avoid any knee-jerk cognitive dissonance.

Finally, the viewpoints displayed in the books comes from a particular character and is not necessarily that of the author's. The author seeks to display flaws, growth and human nature on many levels, and hopes that you will analyse the character of the protagonist without adopting any negative behaviours from them.

Merry part, and merry meet again.

THE SILVER ICE HAIR

THE DINING HALL

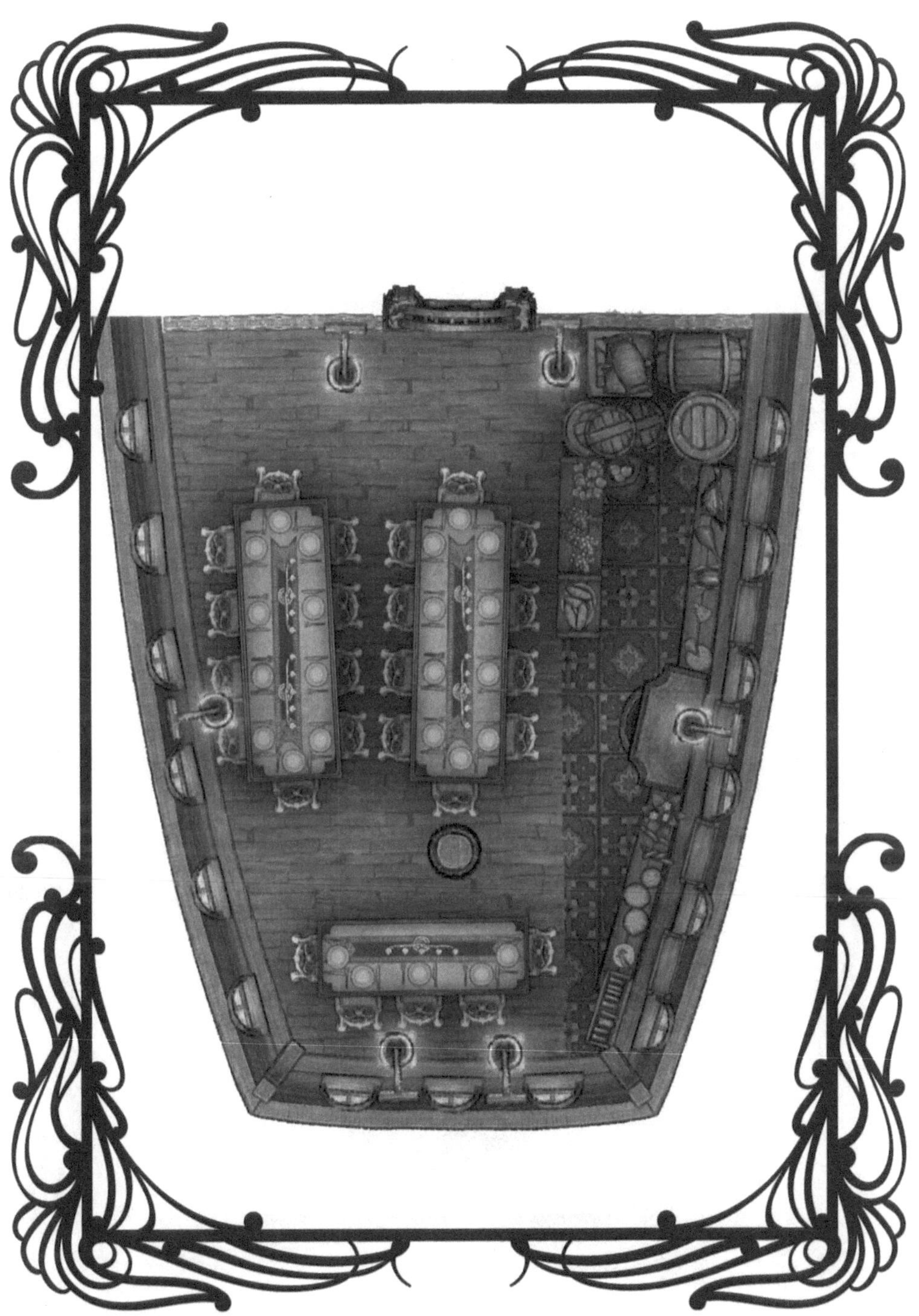

THE PASSENGER CABINS

THE CREW QUARTERS

THE HULL

CHAPTER 1

The Lady and the Nail

Wolflock felt like he had been splashed with a bucket of ice. He couldn't comprehend what he was looking at. The twisted bundle of clothing and limbs at the bottom of the hull stairs looked more like a mangled sculpture than a real person.

His mind squirmed like worms through mud, trying to grasp what was before him.

Parihaan.

She was at the bottom of the stairs. She arched back too far. One leg twisted out to the side and the other was bent under her. One of her arms looked like it had a second elbow from the way her shoulder had contorted. It was her face that chilled him, though. Her head was thrown backwards, and a sliver of her yellow eyes stared back up at him.

He couldn't look.

His throat clenched and his stomach jolted. What was he meant to do?

He crushed his eyes closed and took a breath.

"Help," he croaked, grasping at the wall for support.

Then he heard her.

Parihaan groaned.

His eyes snapped open, unable to move off her. "HELP!" He shouted. Did she really just move? Was she alive? "SOMEBODY COME! QUICKLY! HELP!"

His body started shaking from scene before him. He wanted to run but his legs felt like jelly. Every time he moved he felt the blood in his veins crack like ice.

She groaned again and one of her warped arms dropped to her side. The movement startled him so much that he fell backwards onto the stairs leading up from the landing.

In a flash, the scene was seared into his memory. The railing along the landing and the stairs, the scratches on the floor. The glittering glass shards. The lack of blood. The patterns in the dust on the ground.

The dust. There were shoeprints in the dust. Two sets fresher than his own. One was floral print; one was worn and flat. He looked by his hand on the bottom stair and saw a third, angled in a diamond shape that never made it to the landing. Three people had been down here. But when? Why?

As his eyes followed the pattern of the shoes, he saw the first step down to where Parihaan laid. A huge splinter stuck out from the top step.

"PLEASE! SOMEBODY! HELP!" he cried, trembling. He was about to be sick.

"Wha's the matter, lad?" Grogen's heavy footsteps came up to the top of the stairs and creaked on the planks as he came down to the quivering boy. "Did ya fall? Is anything broken?"

Wolflock shook his head and pointed down the stairs. He gripped Grogen's shirtsleeve. The coarse warm fabric brought him an untold amount of comfort.

"By Houl..." Grogen breathed.

"She-She's alive."

"I don't think she is lad."

"I saw her move! I heard her!" Wolflock begged, clutching Grogen's shirt.

"Let me get another set of hands and we'll 'ave a look, aye? Stay right here."

Grogen tore himself away, but Wolflock grabbed his trouser leg. "D-don't leave me!"

The giant crewman looked back, his big brown eyes filled with concern, yet his mouth twisted into an uncertain grimace.

"Lockie, you listen 'ere, lad. You need to stay 'ere for a moment. I'll be back before you know it. Hold your arms tight and squeeze ya eyes shut. I'll be back before you take ten breaths."

With a reluctant nod, Wolflock gripped his own forearms and closed his eyes. The scene formed behind his eyelids with absolute clarity. If he just kept his mind on the details of the landing... maybe... just maybe he wouldn't see Parihaan's broken form.

There were the distinct footprints, he thought to himself as he focused on every minute details. The pathway where the thoroughfare of people trod daily and the thicker dust along the edges. Tiny grains of dirt and sand were flung from the two most predominant footprints. Fabric strands caught in the wood on the wall. They were from Parihaan's hijab. The railing had smudges on it. A glint of silver streaked the rail as well. Different to the grey wood. It was paint. Wet paint. But just a smear. Then there was the splinter.

No... Not a splinter.

It was a nail. The broad flat top was unmistakable, even though the darkness tried to hide it. It shouldn't be there. It served no purpose there. Why would there be a nail at the top of the stairs? It was a hazard. What was it doing there?

Wolflock's piercing blue eyes opened as he stared at the scene he'd pieced back together in his mind. The jutting piece of metal wasn't a ship nail. It was far too small. Was it a finishing nail from a painting?

He had to know. But it was so close to where he'd see Parihaan. He couldn't bear looking at her. What if he moved low to the ground or tried to grab it without looking? The crew would stomp all over it. What if they stepped on it? What if it was important?

Hearing Grogen and another crew member coming back down, Wolflock acted without thinking. He slunk along the floor and snatched at the nail, keeping himself as far away from the top stair as he could. His hands shook as he fumbled to cram it into his pocket before Grogen picked him up and bear hugged him to his barrel of a chest.

"It's alright, lad. It's alright. Shh. We're 'ere now. Don' you worry."

Hognut and Goden walked past and spoke in low tones. It was all a bit hazy for a few moments. Wolflock resisted his mind trying to go down those stairs. Grogen's broad arms equally suffocated and comforted him, making it easier to keep a grip on his reactions.

"What's going on down there?" Captain Blutro shouted from the top of the stairs.

"There's been an accident, sir." Grogen called over Wolflock's black hair.

"Is that Mr Felen? Are you injured?"

"Not 'im, Captain. It's Parihaan."

"She's alive!" Goden called out as Hognut analysed her. Wolflock caught a glimpse of her misshapen form but turned his face away as he felt his stomach lurch.

"I'll get the doctor," Captain Blutro affirmed.

"Can ya walk, lad?" Grogen gave Wolflock's arms a squeeze.

He nodded and the hulking crewman led him upstairs and sat him down in his cabin. Other passengers started to come out to gawk.

"I'll fetch ya some tea in a moment, but ya should have sommit a bit stronger first. I'll see if Nan Ji has medicine."

He could only nod. His whole body felt numb as he started to shiver. As he looked around his own neat and tidy cabin all he could see was the dust, the footprints, the handprints, the smear of silver, the jutting nail, and...

Wolflock swallowed. He had to get it out of his head. He couldn't think until it was out. Without another thought he pulled out his desk chair, startling himself with the scraping noise it made on the wooden floor. *Was it always that loud?*

Grabbing his notebook, ink and quill, he began jotting down every detail. Halfway through his first sentence he remembered the note in his pocket.

P.
When you get to Krieger Zwerg, make sure the
goods get on board. Someone will meet you in Creast for
pick up. The boss will be furious if you drink it all again
like last time.
Don't mess up.
A.

It was messy from his shaking hand, but he got it down, ignoring the people running to the hull and on high alert to those leaving it. After a page of notes and the beginning of his shoe print sketching, a knock at his door made him cut a line of ink across three words.

"Lockie?" Mothy spoke softly, "I have some tea for

you."

Wolflock left the book open for the ink to dry and turned his chair to see his friend.

"Thank you." His voice came out much stronger than he felt.

Mothy's grey eyes seemed to scan him. *What was he looking for?*

The blond boy set the mug down on the desk and pulled out the second blanket from the overhead storage, throwing it around Wolflock's shoulders. Instantly, he felt relieved. He couldn't believe how cold he'd gotten. *Was there a draft?*

"How are you feeling?"

Wolflock didn't have the words. He opened his mouth, shook his head, and closed it. His gut writhed at his foolishness. Before either of them could speak, Captain Blutro appeared at the door.

"Ah. Good. You're being looked after. They're about to bring her up, Mr Felen. I suggest you stay here. I know it's difficult, but I'm going to have to come and speak to you in a moment. We must know what happened while it is fresh in your mind. Remain in your cabin and I will be back shortly. Look after him, Mothy."

As Captain Blutro spoke Wolflock picked up his tea, refusing to make eye contact with the stern man.

"Aye, aye, Captain."

Wolflock watched the amber liquid in the mug ripple from his trembling hands. He couldn't sit still. He had to get the shakes out. Without tasting the tea, he put it down and stood up, moving to the door.

"Hey! Wait!" Mothy protested.

Wolflock stopped at the entrance and wouldn't budge as his friend tried to tug him back into the room. He had to see. He didn't know what he had to see, but he had to see. Hognut and Goden carefully carried a rudimentary pole and cloth stretcher with a thin grey sheet drawn up to her chin and closed her eyes. Wolflock didn't feel as horrified seeing her twisted form as he did earlier, but his eyes ached to look somewhere else. It appeared everyone had heard the odd commotion of the crew and him yelling, and they had assembled at their doors to satiate their curiosities. Wolflock's eyes scanned each person, but their features seemed strangely warped. It was as if someone had outlined their features with charcoal. Was it the light?

Yifi, Fuhji and Froderyk weren't anywhere to be seen. Wolflock wondered if they would still be in the dining hall. Surely, they had nothing to do with this. In the rooms across from him, he could see Veluse, Yifi's closed door, the twins Bleen and Faleen, Tanni, and Nu.

Veluse's long brown hair was tucked into a silk nightcap with delicately frilled edges. He was in his nightgown, his bright brown eyes blinking rapidly as he stared at the procession. It was just too much blinking for Wolflock to think it was normal.

He saw Bleen and Faleen nodding solemnly to one another as if they knew this would happen all along. Had they simply been observant, or had they read that in her fortune? He'd never seen them interact with Parihaan. Their solemnity didn't sit right with him. Tanni held her hand over her mouth in fright. Wolflock saw tears well in her big dark eyes and he realised that she might very well be reminded of her own husband's passing.

As the crewmen brought Parihaan into her room, Nan Ji stood back from her door and called to Nu.

"*Nǚ'ér. Wánquán ànzhào wǒ de zhǐshì lái duìdài zhège nǚrén.*"

Wolflock reeled back as Nu practically skipped past him, a smile suppressed on her lips. *Why was she so happy? Why was she trying to hide it?*

He couldn't draw the threads of his mental web together as his mind was filled with noise, but in that moment, that thread stood out to him.

Parihaan's room was three down from his. Between them was Stra's room, which the door remained closed to, and Haatji's room. The elegant woman wore a purple satin headscarf and pyjamas under a shimmering dressing gown. She was still wearing her black curly toed shoes with gold beads from earlier. He couldn't see her face, but he could tell that she was trying to hide as much of herself behind the door while being as frozen as stone. Was she shaking too?

To Wolflock's left was Mothy's room, Dlumi, and the empty Kifalme sister's room. Ungul and Uhnha's door was closed, but a light was creeping under the doorway. Dlumi seemed completely perplexed by the whole situation and asked Tanni who was under the sheet.

"Come now, that's enough. Come and sit back down," Mothy insisted, steering Wolflock back into his room.

Wolflock sat back at his desk and began scribbling again.

"Come on, Lockie. I meant to bed. Not to work."

"I have to get it out of my head, Mothy. I don't know what's happening to me," he stammered, snapping the end of his quill. His gut was still twisting like it was filled with worms made of air.

Mothy pressed his upper arms through the blanket. "It's shock. Ma and I helped a lot of the family with it. Take a deep slow breath for one... two... three... four... five. And hold it. One... two... three... four... five. And out... two... three... four... five. Do it with me this time."

Wolflock huffed, putting his hands by his sides, and following Mothy's excruciatingly slow instructions. After the second round of breathing, Wolflock's shoulders relaxed and his stomach unknotted. They went through five cycles and his mind felt like leaves that had gradually fallen back to the earth. Settled.

"That's better. You're back to your normal colour now."

"My colour?"

"Yeah. You're not as white as a ghost anymore."

Mothy let go of his shoulders and sat on the desk while Wolflock dug out another quill from the drawer. His thoughts came in far more cohesive waves again.

"You've never seen something like that before?"

Wolflock shook his head, pausing his pen for a moment.

"S'well enough." His friend's slender hand gripped his shoulder in support.

"I've been to hospitals and Plugh was attacked during the war. I saw amputees and people with eye patches. Nothing like that though." Wolflock paused for a moment and looked up at his friend. "You've seen that before though, haven't you?"

"Aye... I have."

Wolflock didn't press the topic. He didn't want to feel worse than he already did. They stayed silent for quite some time before Mothy gestured back to the mug.

"It will go cold. Go on. Stra said it will be bitter from the jasmine if you let it sit too long."

"Stra?"

"He added some herbs to Nan Ji's sleep tonic to help everyone rest better after the altercation earlier."

Hearing that this was Nan Ji's sleep potion, Wolflock had no desire to drink it. The old physician hated Parihaan and had never given her an ounce of leniency. Wolflock cradled the mug but refused to drink. Mothy continued to look at him expectantly until Captain Blutro interrupted them.

"Are you well, Mr Felen?"

"Fine, Captain." He avoided the silver haired man's eyes again.

"May I have that word with you now?" Wolflock knew he was only asking to be polite. He didn't really have a choice in the matter. "I need you to walk me through every detail. I just want to confirm this was an accident and not anything more."

Wolflock's mouth twitched as the word '*accident*' felt like an itch in his mind. His faculties were not as sharp as they were when he first saw Parihaan at the bottom of the hull. *Was it the drinking alcohol still affecting him? Was it the lack of sleep? Was it the horrific scene wearing off?*

"You found me coming out of the hull after I'd been investigating the smuggling of drinking alcohol, then we went upstairs to see Parihaan fighting with Geagle, Nan Ji, Nu and Haatji. Parihaan ran off and Grogen dunked me in a barrel of water." He nodded behind the captain as Grogen appeared to listen as well. "I spoke for a while with Yifi, Fuhji, Froderyk and Grogen. Haatji was there too but she left before me. Grogen told me to go and collect the last of the drinking alcohol and give it to you, but I thought I'd find Parihaan and send her to the dining room first."

"He seemed so upset, Cap'in. I couldn't stand seein' 'im so put out, so I sent 'im to get the booze and give 'im somethin' to do. Then I thought I best go down and make sure he doesn' get inta any more mischief and offend Miss Parihaan. He could get 'imself into a altercation o'sorts, I thought. Took me a few minutes to be decided, but I thought it was for the best."

"Your judgement was impeccable," Captain Blutro nodded to his crewmate.

"I couldn't find her..."

Wolflock began running the nail of his thumb over

the zig zag pattern carved into the nail, remembering fractures of the night before. *Mothy wasn't in his room. Nu just dashed into her family's cabin. He crashed into Haatji as he came downstairs...*

"Goden was asleep outside her door..."

The dust. The footprints. The threads of fabric clinging to the wall. The silver paint...

"I decided to come downstairs into the hull to finish my task and see if she was down here."

The broken lantern. The twisted form at the bottom of the stairs.

"And then I called out for help."

"Did you see anyone coming or going from the hull?" Captain Blutro leaned forward and raised his bushy eyebrows.

"No. I didn't see anyone after I reached the crew quarters."

With a sigh, the Captain stood up straight. "Very well. As far as I can see, she snuck passed Goden to fetch whatever was left of the drinking alcohol. As she was already poisoned from it and dizzy, it is clear that she simply toppled down the stairs. Thank you for your explanation, Mr Felen. Now, please rest up-"

"But Captain!" Wolflock started, not realising he had stood up. "Other people were down there. There were at least two other people down there before I found her. There are shoe prints and handprints and silver paint!"

Captain Blutro frowned. "Mr Felen, I appreciate your concern, but all evidence and your very description points to her falling by accident. I can't allow for anymore disharmony on my ship through a mere speculation. What's done is done. Don't trouble yourself any further on this matter."

"But-"

"Mothy," Captain Blutro turned and stepped through the door, "why hasn't he drunk his tea yet?"

Grogen nodded to them and left with the Captain as Mothy rushed and took Wolflock's cup.

"Come on, Lockie. This is going to make you feel better."

"I don't like sedatives."

Mothy pressed his lips tightly together, tilting the mug in his hands, "That's fair. I don't think it's a strong one. It's just for nightmares. Lavender and that kind of thing."

"Yes. But it's Nan Ji."

"Oh, he's fine." Mothy waved his hand. "Just..."

"Horrible? Rude? Mean? Arrogant?"

"I was going to say determined?"

Wolflock scoffed. "Just because you like his

daughter doesn't mean you have to like him."

Mothy chuckled and shrugged. "You don't have to drink it. Would you like food?"

"I think I just want to finish my notes and get to sleep. I feel like when we had to swab the deck, but as if we did it five times over."

"Also, fair. I'll let you sleep, but if you need me for anything at all, just come and flick my ear."

Wolflock smirked and waved back to Mothy as he departed. He swivelled in his seat and checked the bottom of his shoes for the pattern in the tread before writing down the clues. He had to collect the data. That included his own shoes too. He had to be thorough. That was all he could cling to right now.

Dust thick along the edges of the landing where no one normally stepped.

Freshest imprints from Grogen's bare feet and my own straight-lined shoes.

Two sets of oddly angled prints smearing the thick layers of dust to the side.

Then there was the one shoe print on the last step before the landing. Had someone had come down the stairs, seen the scene, then gone back up?

A smear in the dust showed feet that moved quickly, scattered the particles of dirt away.

The one with a slight heel and big flat shoe nails was up against the wall.

Floral print was backed to the bannister.

Floral print tread had tiny fine nails and a sharp cut to the leather.

Bigger nailed shoes had a jagged rough cut.

Neither had pressed their weight on their toes. Can't tell how big the shoe size is.

Looking over his notes and the sketches he'd made of the three shoe prints, he began to see little details he hadn't before. Two nails were missing on the outer ball of the left poorly cut shoes. One nail was missing from the right shoe but one in the heel looked loose. It hadn't left perfect circles like the others, but a crooked smear.

Wolflock reached into his pocket and withdrew the nail. It was a shoe nail. This was the missing nail. It was missing from the outer edge of the right shoe. Why would the outer nails be coming out though?

He stood up and rolled his foot around, trying to see what kind of pressure might wiggle the nails free from the outside. After a few moments and a near slip, he determined that it would take some heavy wobbling to cause those particular nails to wriggle free. It would have to be someone who stumbles often. Someone who might be regularly intoxicated. Someone like Parihaan.

In his mind he began to see the scene on the landing. As if he were watching shadows in his mind, he saw Parihaan run down the stairs and stop at the landing and lean on the wall, her headscarf catching in the wood and tearing a few threads loose. Someone else came down. He could nearly hear the muted arguing. Did Parihaan push first or did the other person? Either way, the floral shoed person was pushed to the railing, gripping onto it to steady themselves. How did they leave a streak of silver paint though? They pushed Parihaan back to the wall. Then something happened and Parihaan fell down the stairs...

As Wolflock looked at the zig zag pattern indented in the leather still stuck to the nail he wondered...

Did she really fall? Or was she pushed?

20

CHAPTER 2

A Night of Messages

Wolflock got changed into his pyjamas and had thought that now that he had all the evidence from the hull written down, he would be able to sleep. Everyone else seemed to be sleeping, so why couldn't he? He tossed and turned for hours and finally gave up. He laid there looking up at the darkness. He felt embarrassed at how he'd responded to seeing Parihaan. He'd frozen. He could have helped her. What if he'd gotten to her and been able to wake her up? He didn't get to tell her the message from the others. He didn't get to tell her that she had people who cared.

For the first time since he had come onto the ship Wolflock felt alone. Truly alone. The injustice that Parihaan had people who cared, even if they didn't know her that well, and yet no one had been able to tell her in time, made his heart feel like it was thrown in the snow. It left him with the same pain that he'd felt when his father... Wolflock shook the thoughts out of his head. He wasn't going to think about that. He chose to travel to Mystentine University. No one forced him. He chose it. And he'd never damn well let anyone think anything different.

He swung his legs out of bed and began pacing in his room. Surely, he missed something. Surely there was some detail he was missing that would magically wake her up and he could just tell her that she had friends and it would reverse the whole thing. What if the nail wasn't hers? That would put a whole new spin on everything.

He snatched up the nail and carefully opened his cabin door. The hallway was dark except for a light blue glow from the settled fairy dust lanterns. The eerie glow mixed with the sleepy silence of the ship made it feel like some strange magic had taken hold of the vessel.

It felt as if he was somewhere he wasn't meant to be on a spiritual level, but instead of recoiling from it, it made him smile. He stepped past Haatji's room and stopped. She was talking. No. Humming? He pressed his ear to the door for a moment and listened. Her lispy voice was chanting something in her native tongue from Uluken. Every now and then she'd gasp and sob, then continue her chanting. Wolflock wondered if she was praying as he stepped away. As he came to Parihaan's closed door he took the fairy dust lantern from the wall; he had forgotten to bring a light from his own room. Silently, he slipped into the room and jostled the lantern just enough to bring up a little of the blue light. He didn't know if she'd wake up at any moment and he didn't want to startle her.

Her room was as bare as Mothy's apart from a few trinkets on the desk. A mirror, some perfumed hair oil, an old stone comb, and a small jewellery box sat on the polished wood. Wolflock looked around and saw the window was cracked open; he could still hear Haatji chanting in her own room. Parihaan had also left her key in the wardrobe lock.

Trusting, he thought to himself.

As he lifted the light higher, he saw her sleeping form. His gut yanked inside him. She wasn't sleeping. She was too still. Nu had straightened her out and she was laying on her back, her headscarf removed. He hadn't seen her without her hijab before. She was objectively average looking to him, but her long black hair was extraordinary. He surmised that Nu had put it in a loose braid to keep it out of the way, but it also kept it neat and tidy. The braid ran over her shoulder and almost down to her hip. It gleamed in the light with a perfect sheen that many people would pay many deimas for. He saw her left cheek was slightly swollen compared to the right and there was a thin line of silver that would have been invisible had the light not shone on its metallic reflectiveness. Her hands, neatly folded on her stomach on top of the blanket, were dirtied with a dark stain. He peered closer, holding his breath for a moment. It was black and reddish. Like blood.

Wolflock touched the knuckle of his index finger to his chin as he thought. Had Parihaan scratched her attacker? Someone had been there when she fell, he was sure of that. Did they have wounds from their fight?

Nu had prepared a strong-smelling cushion by her patient's face. He could tell it was to keep her breathing soundly as he felt his own breath deepen when he smelt it. An empty cup of herbs also sat by her bedside. He didn't know if it would help, but as he collected all the data he hoped something about her fall would become clear.

Remembering his purpose, Wolflock moved to her wardrobe and unlocked it with the little silver key. Her clothes were hanging untidily on the wooden coat hangers, some had fallen to the floor. He set the lantern down inside the cupboard and picked them up, looking over each piece. They were old. Quite old. The hems were frayed; some of the pockets had holes. Some were worn in places usually hidden by the many layers she normally wore.

After tidying her clothes, he knelt down and looked over her shoes. She had two pairs. One set was immaculate. Barely used at all and sewn with dazzling blue glass beads. *Event shoes*, he nodded.

The other pair were worn, orange curl toed shoes, ones he'd seen her wear everywhere else. The soles were thin and, as he picked them up, he could see parts of them were peeling off. The left shoe had two nails missing and matched the prints he'd noted earlier. The holes were large and smoothed over. They'd been missing for a while. The right shoe was missing one nail from the outer edge from a similar hole as the left nails. Another was loose, and the heel nail was torn free, leaving a gash from the heel towards the toe. He pulled out the nail with the zig zag imprint on it. It was the same leather.

She'd been backed against the wall and had pushed someone to the railing. She'd fallen down the stairs. But who was the person wearing the floral print shoes?

As he pondered the question, the lantern dimmed. The darkness helped him think.

Or at least, it would have if Parihaan's door hadn't opened.

Was Nu coming to check on her? Was there a schedule to make sure she was still stable?

The person crept into the room behind Wolflock. His eyes had adjusted to the darkness better now that he'd been crouching in it for some time, and he could see they were wearing a hooded cloak.

Odd... He stood up, lantern in hand, but it gave off no light.

Perhaps I should let them know I'm here. Or perhaps I should just duck out. I'm not meant to be in here anyway.

He stepped towards the door, watching the person approach Parihaan's side.

It might be Geagle. I definitely don't want to hear him pine for her. Wolflock's left hand found the door.

The dark figure raised their right arm. They were holding something.

A long spiralling knife.

"Hey!" Wolflock shouted, shaking the fairy dust lantern as he raised it.

The light flushed the room and the person about to stab Parihaan raised their cloaked arm, shielding their face. The light burned into Wolflock's eyes and he blinked rapidly, trying to see clearly again. Before he could say or do anything, the assailant rushed forward. Wolflock drew the lantern up and heard it smash against their knife.

Did they just try to stab me!?

The hooded figure growled, grabbed his arm, and hurled him to the ground behind them. Wolflock crashed into Parihaan's bedside table, rattling the draws free, and felt his arm hit something sharp. He whipped his face around to see the figure vanish from the room. Using the open draw to scramble to his feet, he ran after them.

They must have run onto the deck! He thought furiously, dashing up the stairs and scanning the deck. His piercing blue eyes were wide and wildly searching for any movement. Nothing.

Kolor the half vampire was pulling rigging and Captain Blutro was steering at the helm.

"Kolor! Did anyone just come up here?" he asked, panting. She finished tying off a rope and scratched her bald head with her long nails. "Not this evening, Mr Felen, but I only just came here."

"They would have been wearing a cloak. A dark cloak?"

"Nothing, sir. Sorry."

With a sigh, he shook his head and waved her off, descending back beneath the deck. Someone had gone into Parihaan's room and sought to kill her. He reached his own door and placed his hand on the handle. He couldn't go in. What if they came back? What if in his chase they'd already gone back in?

He steeled his nerves and flung open her door.

Nothing.

Just the remnants of the smashed fairy dust lantern and the toppled bedside table. Wolflock sighed and went about cleaning things up again. He mostly kicked the glass shards to the edge of the room and collected her few personal items from the bedside table. In the dim remaining light he found a small leather-bound book. It was written in the language of Uluken, but it looked to him like a diary. Perhaps someone onboard could help him translate it?

He couldn't leave her unprotected though. Not when she was in immediate danger. She had no way to defend herself.

He sighed, pocketed the book in his dressing gown, then took up his sentinel for the night sitting in the hallway with his back pressed to her door. No one would get to her without getting passed him first.

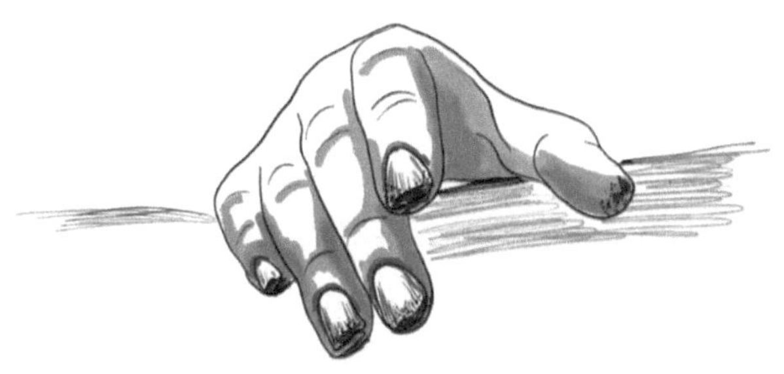

CHAPTER 3

A Nü Patient

Wolflock could see the hull stairs ahead of him. He felt as if he were floating a foot in the air at the very start of the landing. The dust on the landing was undisturbed. A floorboard creaked and a few grains of dirt flicked to the wall. Was someone down here? He saw a sweaty handprint appear on the railing just before the second flight and heard a woman crying. Her dry gasps came in uneven heaves, then thick sobs.

"Parihaan?"

He saw a few threads of her headscarf tear free as a splinter of wood from the wall caught her. He could tell she was leaning on the wall, invisible but for the traces she left behind. He could hear her trying to compose herself.

His head felt like it was underwater. He looked around. Someone was about to come down. He knew it. The hull's walls were gone except for the one at the landing. The room sat heavy in a huge silver spiderweb.

Where is the spider? Was all he could think.

A floorboard creaked and he heard someone talking as they descended the stairs. He saw no figure, but dust from the bottom of the stairs showered down into the spiderweb abyss. Their tone... they were berating her. Wolflock knew that tone all too well. He felt anger seething up inside his chest.

The footprints appeared in the dust. The voice was joined by Parihaan's. She talked in a garbled, underwater distortion, but he heard her trying to aggressively defend herself.

The floral shoe prints appeared, and the side railing creaked. Parihaan had shoved the person away. A dull thump hit the wall as Parihaan was shoved against it, her poorly made shoes leaving their uneven prints. The pair wrestled for a few moments. Wolflock could feel the electricity of the fight crackle against him.

"Stop!" he cried out, but he felt like his body was moving through treacle. Weighted and slow, it took all his effort to just raise his arm. He was so close. He could catch her. He could stop her falling.

As he reached the top of the stairs, he heard the rolling thuds. He looked down. Ice filled his veins.

"Wolflock?"

Wolflock jerked awake and threw his head back into Parihaan's door. Nu touched his arm. It hurt.

"Wolflock, are you well?"

He didn't know where he was at first. Why was he in the hallway?

"I... I'm fine."

"You're bleeding."

"What?"

Nu pulled his sleeve up and revealed a long thin gash down his forearm. It must have happened when he fell on the smashed lantern last night. He hadn't even felt it.

"You are not well. Come in and I will make sure this is mended before I treat my patient."

He was too tired to argue and his back ached from sleeping in such an awful position all night. The fresh dawn light hadn't even lifted its sleepy face yet.

Why is Nu awake?

She sat him down at Parihaan's desk and took off the arm of his quilted maroon dressing gown. He'd cut right through to the arm of his grey pyjamas and they were soaked with blood.

"This is going to sting. The blood has clotted to the fabric. How did you do this?" she asked as she dabbed his sleeve with a warm damp towel.

"I... I fell on a lantern."

"You could not sleep. You should have drunk father's sleep tonic. It is one of his best remedies."

"Mmm..."

She hadn't seen the shards of the fairy dust lantern he'd pushed into the corner yet. He wouldn't have to answer too many questions.

Wolflock winced as she peeled the sleeve away and dressed it with a moist sachet of herbs and a clean white bandage.

"It is not deep, and no glass is in it. You are very lucky. Why were you sitting outside my patient's room?"

"I..." He thought about telling her the truth, but the memory of her smiling yesterday stopped him. "I thought I heard a noise and didn't want... I didn't want to have her wake up without getting the message I was meant to tell her."

Nu massaged the cushion soaked with oils to bring the smell out again and took Parihaan's pulse. "You are a strange person, Wolflock. Very strange. Wait for a moment. I must prepare her herbs and I will get you some too. We must stop any infection."

The moment Nu left the room, Wolflock went back to his own cabin and picked up his quill. Unlike the gigantic spider web in his dream, his own mental web was in tatters. He had to get his thoughts in order. He had to know who he was looking for.

Who was the second person on the landing last night?

He had to make a timeline to see who the most likely suspects were.

He knew it had to have happened within the time Parihaan had run from her altercation with everyone on the top deck and before he had gone down to the hull to find her. He began scratching down lines, times, and locations to place the crew and company. That period of time was the changeover for the day and night shift crew, so none of them were in the cabins sleeping. That meant that there were no witnesses amongst the crew that could verify who had gone down after Parihaan.

He ruled out Grogen, Yifi, Fuhji and Froderyk. Slavidus was at the helm waiting for Captain Blutro to changeover, so it couldn't have been him. Didi, Gege and Tinni's shoes were far too small to be the prints present on the landing. Goden was asleep at Parihaan's door, so another person crossed off. As he went through the whereabouts of the crew and company, he narrowed down his search to those he hadn't seen otherwise engaged during that hour.

Haatji had seemed flustered, Nan Ji was nowhere to be found, Nu had just dashed back into her room, Geagle was also absent, along with Captain Blutro. Mothy was also not in his cabin, but he knew it wasn't him. Mothy wouldn't have been capable of this. Neither was Veluse or Tanni.

He paused, his pen dripping a speck of ink onto his journal page. That wasn't a good enough reason. Just because he thought he knew someone didn't mean he could rule them out. Everyone was a suspect until he obtained more conclusive evidence. He ruled up a new page with the ship's crew and company written down the left hand side. The next columns were labelled 'Evidence', 'Alibi', 'Motive', and 'Conclusion'. Next to each name he drew an empty circle for suspects and an empty square for unlikely suspects. Anyone proven innocent had their name crossed out.

Satisfied he had a few leads to follow, Wolflock sat back in his chair, catching a glimpse of Nu rolling her dark almond shaped eyes at him. His door had been left open so he wasn't surprised she found him.

"You are so disobedient."

Wolflock snorted. "No, I'm not."

"And stubborn. Give me your arm."

He rolled his bright blue eyes back at her and held out his arm as if it were the most troublesome thing he could ever be asked to do. She carefully checked him over before sitting down a tincture of bitter smelling herbs on his desk.

"I know you do not like my father, but he would not hurt you. He does not like your disrespect, but he is a good doctor. He took an oath to never cause intentional harm to a patient."

Wolflock didn't meet her eye. "He wasn't being a good doctor when he refused to treat Parihaan."

"He is stubborn. You have that in common. My father thinks that all women are very fragile. My mother died from a sickness he could not heal, so now he is always too cautious. He does not want to be responsible for a woman dying again. Parihaan also did not treat him with respect. He did not like her much."

Wolflock's eyes narrowed and he followed her back to her patient's room, watching her suspiciously as she worked.

"She wasn't your favourite person on the ship either, was she, Nü?"

She stopped and blinked up at him in surprise. "Pardon?"

"You definitely didn't like her after what she said to you about your mother and your intelligence, did you?" How could someone smile last night? Her little hands matched Parihaan's cheek and she could even have shoes to match the dust prints. They were certainly a more feminine design. Had she gone downstairs for herbs and taken an opportunity to get rid of the woman who was so keen on assaulting her father and her honour? Had Parihaan provoked Nü again? It was certainly feasible as Nu often went downstairs to gather more ingredients for her father and her brother.

"It is a poor custom to speak ill of someone unwell," she stiffened, her demeanour becoming frosty.

"Where were you last night after Parihaan left the deck?" he snarled.

Right on cue, Mothy appeared at his side, yawning. "You're up early? Oh. Did...did I walk in on something?" He rubbed his eyes and looked between his friends.

Nü's eyes narrowed dangerously, "I was on the deck watching the stars with my brothers and the twins staying out of the way. Mothy was with us for a time." Mothy nodded as he moved between them. "I would like to change the subject now."

"I bet you would..." Wolflock snorted.

Mothy smiled brightly and clapped Wolflock on the

shoulder a little too firmly. "You, my good Lockie, are a little ball of sunshine, aren't you? Come now! We're all friends. We should rejoice that every day we draw closer to our destination. Besides! Look what I got."

Mothy pulled out three little cakes from his pocket, wrapped in one of the dining hall's silver trimmed kerchiefs. They were perfect little domes with a squished custard swirl on top and a dusting of icing sugar. They looked mouth-watering.

"Where on Pelaia did you get those from?" Wolflock's eyes went wide.

He didn't normally have a sweet tooth but looking at these cakes made him think of the delicate pastries the cook made back home.

"I saw Matroos making them with Grogen yesterday during their changeover. They're custard filled!"

"These look far too special. We haven't been served cakes like this since we've been on board. How did you get them?" Wolflock asked as he took the one Mothy passed to him.

"Oh, you know. I just thought there was a few extra on the side of the tray and they wouldn't be any good to whoever Matroos was making them for. I mean if it was for the crew then he'd made far too many."

"You stole them?" Wolflock snorted and took a bite.

The perfectly soft pastry melted between his teeth and the burst of thick custard flooded his mouth with pure joy. It was exceptionally delicious.

"I like to say I helped distribute them. It's good to see you eat finally."

Wolflock ignored him and looked back at Parihaan.

"Nu, are you going to clean her nails?"

"I was going to bath her today with an ointment to help the swelling go down."

"Ah, so you've seen her cheek then?"

"Yes." She looked back at him from the corner of her eye.

"I wonder, is that different from the other bruises and bumps she has?"

"It is going down faster than the other places and has not bruised so deeply."

"As if she's been slapped. I wonder what would prompt someone to do such a thing." He walked around Nu as she knelt on the ground beside her patient, pretending to analyse Parihaan's cheek. "I'm sure someone who was as insulted as you were would like to slap her. Look, it's even about the same size as your hand."

"You are such a temperamental friend, Wolflock!" She flared up, jumping up and balling her fists. "I know what you are doing. I am no fool. You think I pushed her down the stairs. You think I struck her. Yes, she insulted my mother, my intelligence, my family. Yes, she is rude and cruel and stupid. I am not happy for her." Her low voice had pitched higher in rage. "I am not cruel. I did smile yesterday, but I thought you would have been smart enough to know why. I thought we were friends enough to know each other."

She glanced back at Mothy and her shoulders slumped. "This is the first time my father has ever asked me to treat a patient. He believed that I would be able to treat her well enough to bring our family esteem amongst those on the ship. He believed I could at least make her comfortable. But I am going to heal her. I am going to show him that I am just as worthy as my brothers and that I am not fragile. I'm going to do the best job no matter what you think. I am going to give this woman everything I have to make her better."

Wolflock had to step back from her fury. Her passion and determination were undeniable, but it didn't explain why she had gone into her room right before he found Parihaan.

"You're right, Nu. I'm sorry."

Mothy and Nu both jerked in surprise.

"I should know you better. I was just so spooked last night. I saw you go into your cabin just before I found her, and those details are seared into my memory. I think I just feel so powerless if this was truly an accident."

"I understand." She nodded slowly, her eyes drifting over the sleeping woman. "I have seen Father do the exact same thing with his patients before. It can make you a bit too stuck in your path, though. I was on the deck with my brothers and we did not want to go to sleep in the cabin after father had such a spat. I went downstairs to get us a few blankets and pillows so we could be warm and comfortable. That was all. Then before I could finish gathering everything the crew went into a frenzy after you found her."

It made sense. Wolflock felt a little guilty for suspecting Nu, but he was happier that she was able to give him reasons for her innocence.

"You need rest, Lockie." She lowered her voice again and took his arm, feeling his pulse with three fingers at his wrist. "I will make you a special tonic that will help restore you and help you sleep without making you drowsy."

"You're the only one I would trust to do that besides Mothy." He laughed. "The ones your father makes always taste awful."

The three of them chuckled for a while and let the tensions ease.

"So... What is your prognosis, Doctor Nu?" Mothy

smiled and bumped his elbow to hers.

"Hmm? For Parihaan? She will take much longer to heal because her liver and kidneys are so damaged. She hit the back of her head during her fall, so I have to wait for that swelling to go down and then I will make sure her back is not broken. Swelling around the head is more dangerous though. I will treat that first."

Wolflock leaned by the ajar window and watched the oncoming misty river. Through the fog, the trees along the banks were transforming into boulders and it would only be a few hours before they were travelling through the belly of the passage to the country of Shiriling. Watching the landscape helped to clear his thoughts.

As he looked out across the river his suspicions of Nu diminished. Her reason for smiling inappropriately seemed genuine. If her alibi could be corroborated by her brothers or anyone else on deck, that would be the end of it. As she knelt down next to Parihaan he saw the bottom of her shoes. They were made of a thick fabric with tiny little blue birds embroidered on the sides. The stitching left knots as big as a ladybug around the edges of the soles and they had a worn cloud pattern across them.

"How many pairs of shoes do you have, Nu?" he asked.

She closed her eyes and began taking Parihaan's

pulse. "Two. One for smooth floors and one for rough."

Wolflock hummed, making a mental note to check that detail too.

If those pieces of evidence worked in Nu's favour, the most likely culprits that were left were Haatji, Geagle, Nan Ji and possibly Captain Blutro. All had a motive. Haatji was insulted by Parihaan on a cultural level, Geagle had been heartbroken, Nan Ji had been insulted as well, and Captain Blutro knew she had been the one to smuggle alcohol aboard his vessel. Wolflock also didn't know where any of them had been prior to him finding Parihaan. Well... he knew Haatji had been in the passenger cabins, so she would be the first one to further investigate. Perhaps their difference of views on culture would be enough to cause this kind of spat.

One of the crew could have also done this out of sympathy for Geagle, and they also had better access to the hull. He'd have to check their shoes and see if they had matching footprints.

Wolflock had to look at the facts, though. And, in order to do that, he had to examine a few things. Things he doubted anyone would approve of him doing. If he found the floral print shoes, he'd find his key suspect. He pinched his chin in thought, not listening to Mothy try and make Nu laugh. The culprit would have scratches on their upper body. He should definitely keep an eye out for that. Geagle normally wore short sleeves, so seeing fresh scratches on his arms would be easy.

Wolflock looked around. There was something that may be used to help back Geagle into enough of a corner to get answers. But where was it? He moved to Parihaan's cupboard and began searching. It wasn't here.

"Nu? Did you change Parihaan's clothes last night?" he asked, pinching his chin again.

She looked up at him, curiosity glinting in her dark eyes. "Yes. This was the only nightclothes I could find for her to be comfortable in. Why?"

"Did you happen to find a silver flask on her person?"

Nu rose in a smooth motion and moved to the cupboard, moving Mothy aside as he scratched his nose with both hands like a squirrel. "I do not recall, but if I had it would be in here." she started searching through Parihaan's dress pockets. "What did you need it for?"

"Oh. Nothing. I just saw her with it yesterday is all." He knew if he lingered much longer, he'd have to tell them his plan; Nu would object to him investigating her father and Mothy would object to him blaming anyone for the crime. "I'll see you both later. I'm going to go for a walk before breakfast."

He went back to his own cabin, got dressed into his white shirt, black vest, slacks, and black leather shoes before ascending to the top deck. He was grateful to move around as sleeping on the hard floor had made his backside stiff. As the dim morning sun caressed his sharp features, he stretched out his long arms, glad for the space to move. He walked around the edge of the ship, trailing his fingertips along the polished light grey railing. A white fog hugged the ship as it glided over the silky waters. Occasionally a puff of fog would float across the ship and dissipate before it reached him. He made his way halfway around the deck before he started hearing a high chinking noise. As he rounded the dining hall, he found Grogen and Hognut chiselling a set of large round stones, about the size of a fist. Grogen sat next to a box on the deck that had a large black cloth hanging out of it.

"What are you doing?" Wolflock asked as he approached.

"Lockie?" Grogen's eyes shot up and he stopped chiselling. They looked red from lack of sleep. "What are ye up for, lad?"

"I couldn't sleep. What are you doing?" he asked again.

Grogen shuffled his shoulders. "We... uh... we're preparin' the burial stones. Just in case."

"Ship funerary rights? Fascinating, but a bit premature don't you think?" Wolflock felt his throat tightening as he spoke. He tucked his hands under his arms to try and keep warm.

"Morbid ya mean..." Hognut scoffed and continued chipping away at his own stone.

"I don't think anyone thinks she's gonna wake up lad. Best we be prepared."

Wolflock opened his mouth to protest, but closed it again, biting his cheek. He realised it would be better to try and get information from them now, rather than let them know what his mind was set on. Perhaps they could tell him where everyone was last night instead of him probing the crew and company individually.

"What are the rights for a river or sea burial?"

"It's a old thing, this." Grogen sighed. "The body is wrapped in salt ta keep fishes away until Houl can open his gates and accept the spirit back ta the Great Mother. We're meant to put black candles 'round the body too. The candles keep the spirit in near the body so it don't roam 'round the ship. There's also a black cloth for tha face"

"A black cloth?"

Grogen looked uncomfortable, "It's so she can't see us. Pari didn' live a happy life. She was angry and sad and confused. Her spirit won' be much betta. She might seek vengeance on those who ain't really done 'er no wrong but laid 'er to rest. Poor lass..."

"And the rocks?" Wolflock stepped closer, looked at the ceremonial stones.

"They help keep the body at the floor of the river. Once the spirit has time to be taken by Houl the salt will have been used up by the water and then the fish can 'ave the body without it floatin' up and scarin' folk."

"Circle o' life," Hognut shrugged, finishing his stone and starting another one.

"How long do you think she's going to last?" Wolflock asked, unable to keep a very slight note of nervousness from his voice.

"Who can say? Could be an hour, could be weeks. I'm not a doctor, lad."

Hognut remained stoic and silent, smoking on his pipe.

"Who did you see on your way to the hull last night? I was just hoping no one else saw her and is too shocked to talk about it."

For the first time since Wolflock had known him, Grogen looked suspicious, his eyes narrowed, and his chin lifted.

"All the crew was where they was meant to be. I was in the kitchen 'til I came to get yeh, Geagle was on watch-"

"No 'e wasn't," Hognut grunted, striking a match to relight his pipe before beginning to chisel again.

"What are yeh talkin' 'bout?"

"Geagle wasn' on watch. 'E never does watch. Goes and writes those stupid letters or skips it for a lass."

"Fine," Grogen scoffed. "Geagle was writing letters, Kolor was on deck duties, and Matroos was teachin' all the passengers to name stars. I say teachin' but I reckon she spent most o' her time arguing wit' the Quaretz twins. All the rest o' the crew was on rest and either sleepin' or watchin' stars with 'em."

Wolflock knew for a fact that the crew were not in the sleeping quarters when he went down, so they must have been entertaining themselves on the deck or in the dining hall. It didn't entirely rule them out, but perhaps there was more information he could glean from them.

"Were the Nan family members there?"

"The kids were. Old Nan Ji got an early night."

"So Nu was there?"

"She's your age, lad, so she counts as a kid ta me," Grogen snorted.

"I... uh..." Wolflock thought as fast as he could. Clearly, he didn't have long before they finished their task and went about their normal duties. "Do you need a hand?"

Grogen looked up and then glanced at Hognut, who was staring as if Wolflock was some weird grub.

"Only got two sets o' chisels, lad."

"Oh... What about-"

"What's this about, lad?" Grogen cut him off quite abruptly and stared him with a fearsomeness that made the boy's knees buckle. It was like having a bear stare at him within swiping distance. "No one wants to prepare for the dead 'cept fam'ly. It ain't right. This ain't no game, lad!"

Wolflock threw up his hands defensively. "No! No! I understand that! It's just... well..."

Grogen just stared at him with a deadly coldness.

"Parihaan and I didn't get along and I feel like it was all my fault. I never got the chance to apologise... I just wanted to tell her I'm sorry... She just seemed so... hard done by."

He raised his shoulders around his ears and avoided Grogen's searching eyes. He barely knew the woman at all. Why did he feel like talking about her as if she were already dead was so wrong? Why did he feel anything at all?

Grogen's sighed and hugged Wolflock around the shoulders.

"Ah... lad..." he sighed and glanced at the stones. "Ain't nothing we can do but leave it to the gods."

"Where was everyone last night? I just feel like if I knew where everyone was then maybe it will seem like there was nothing we could have done."

"I understand, lad. I do. When accidents happen, we all feel the same, but no one could have stopped her from tumbling. I think we should jus' be grateful she's alive and hope she either passes easily or Nu works her magic. Go on, now. Ain't nothin' we need a hand with. Get some breakfast. Porridge should be stewed by now."

Wolflock nodded a goodbye to the crewmen and found his way into the unattended kitchen. It was Grogen's day to make breakfast, and he normally took great pride in serving everyone individually with his jolly smile. But today he'd laid out a buffet table.

As Wolflock gathered up an apple, some stewed dates and a bit of porridge, he thought to himself, *Had Grogen been in shock? Is that why Hognut and him were preparing funerary stones together? Or had Grogen been crying and Hognut had been supporting him during his normal rest time in the roster?*

He pushed the thoughts from his head as he sat down. After a few bites of his apple his hands needed something more to do, so he pulled out his notebook from his pocket and grabbed a pencil from the kitchen drawers. He began writing and sketching out his ideas and his mental web in the greatest detail he could, giving the shoe prints a separate page to themselves. He even labelled the important details his sharp memory could carve out.

One by one the crew and company came into the dining hall for their breakfast. They had had buffet breakfasts before, so they knew what to do, but something felt like it was missing without Grogen's friendly demeanour helping serve up the food. Sometimes he even gave terribly mispronounced fancy names for his dishes, making the light at heart laugh.

There was no laughing this morning though.

The sombre slump of his fellow passengers' shoulders and the drag of their feet told him how the shock of last night had injured them too. Were they all feeling guilty? He nodded good morning to several people, and he could tell they wanted to ask him questions, but without a cup of tea yet, it was too early.

As he finished off the sketch of the single shoe print he'd found on the stairs, Veluse and Stra passed behind him. Veluse had been talking to Stra about herbal dyes for fabrics and canvases when he stopped and rested a hand on Wolflock's shoulder.

"My, my, my! Mr Felen! You have a hidden talent. Why did you never tell me you could draw?"

Wolflock turned to see his shapely jawline leaning

over his shoulder. "I... uh... never thought it was a talent. I was taught to draw by my governess when I was a child."

"But, my young master, look at the detail! You have seen so much more. Most people would just draw a blotch. A smudge. A simple line. You! You have taken the very essence of the print. You have seen the depth, the intensity, the sinister meaning that is behind the print!"

Sinister meaning? What on Pelaia was he talking about?

"Uh... thank you? It's mostly so I don't forget it."

"And of course. All artistes seek never to forget their inspirations. If only there was a way that we could capture our very sight and hearts on a page. If only there was a way to take that image so fleeting, so instantaneous. It is the essence of the pulsating moment that is the present."

He had moved a few steps back from Wolflock and thrown his arms about in an exuberant fashion, causing the dining hall to stop and listen to his flourishing speech.

Wolflock flipped the page back without looking, laughed nervously, and turned back to his notebook.

"Oh! I see! You're planning a dance. Well, fear not, my young apprentice-" he rolled the word apprentice for a few seconds, "I will not spoil the fastigium of your choreographing endeavours."

And, like the whirlwind he always was, Veluse blew

away to the next person he could talk at. Stra lingered for a moment, trying to see what Veluse had been in raptures about, then shrugged at the same time as Wolflock did, and moved on as well.

Mothy came to join him with three bowls of porridge, dates, two pears, and a cinnamon drink Haatji had introduced them to a few days ago. As the company began chatting amongst themselves, it nearly felt like the ship was getting back to normal. Wolflock smiled to himself. This would make it easier. If no one knew he was searching for the person who may have pushed Parihaan, then they'd answer his questions more freely. He looked around for Nu, thinking that if she wasn't with her patient, then the person with the knife may return, and he couldn't let that happen.

The light chatter that had risen through the room dwindled into silence as Captain Blutro's heavy footsteps walked down the middle of the tables. Everyone's eyes watched him as he turned a chair around and slowly climbed onto it.

He looked around the room with his stormy grey eyes and made sure every single person had their full attention on him.

"My dear company. Yesterday evening a terrible accident befell one of our own. Although she has not been taken from our lives, she is now straddling this world and the next. Our noble physician on board, Nan Ji, has allowed his beloved daughter to tend to Ms Nebralt's wounds and maintain her spirit until she passes."

Wolflock's nose twitched in irritation. Nu believed she was charged with bringing Parihaan back to full health, not acting as a death doula.

"I would like for us to all take a moment to join together in prayer to wish for Ms Nebralt's easy passing and that Miss Nan Nu is able to facilitate this as well as her father may."

Wolflock scowled, glaring around at the crew and company present. They all joined hands and bowed their heads as if they were already at her funeral. Captain Blutro began to speak an ancient Puinteylien hymn in a low monotone.

"*Blessed be the children of Pelaia, from whom will rise from the Great Mother and sink back into her bosom when fate decides their time. Blessed be the lessons learnt and shared with her, for the tales of our souls feed all. May the sun ever rise over the eternal Summerland that is her heart when night keeps our harmony. May her eyes always fill with love for our endeavours and her arms welcome our souls to keep. So mote it be.*"

As the Captain chanted, Wolflock saw some of the

other passengers mouthing along or humming the words with him. Yifi was sniffing back tears, leaning into Slavidus' arm. Tanni looked pale and frightened, as if the mere thought of death was enough to bring back memories of her deceased husband. Stra's bald head was bowed into polite repose, as were Froderyk and Fuhji.

Wolflock scanned the room thoroughly. Every little expression, every little movement, it was a potential clue, giving away their true feelings. It could be enough to give them away. A little irritated twitch in the fingers, a wrinkled nose trying to hide contempt. His piercing blue eyes locked in on each person in turn.

Geagle was present, and Wolflock could tell his pink face was a few shades paler. His hands shook and his droopy, watery eyes darted around. They met Wolflock's and he refused to back down. Their staring match held for only a few seconds before Geagle bowed his head and stayed very still.

He knew something.

The other crew around the room looked solemn and awkward. Wolflock didn't think they really had it in them to push a passenger down the stairs, but they did have the best access to the hull.

Wolflock looked to the next people, the Nan family. Didi and Gege, Nu's younger brothers, kept their heads bowed, but as children would in this situation, they looked confused and a bit bored. Nan Ji on the other hand, had refused to bow his head. His chin was raised, and his face writhed with hatred.

A powerful response for such a fleeting confrontation.

As Wolflock looked further along the tables at the company, he saw something else that caught his eye.

Haatji had bowed her head only a little and had balled her hands together in front of her heart. Her eyes were shut tight and she was praying furiously. Glittering tears streaked down her cheeks.

Wolflock didn't understand. She hated Parihaan. She'd even struck her. Why was she crying? Was she feeling guilty?

56

CHAPTER 4

A Slew of Crew Shoes

He had to know.

Everyone took their seats at the table nearest the kitchen and he watched Haatji sit diagonally across from him at the second table with the twins, Bleen and Faleen. Wolflock remained standing, eyeing the chairs, the dishes, the jugs of infused tea.

Mothy began lifting the jugs within reach and peered into them. Finally, he blew a raspberry in distaste.

"All bitter ones. Grogen sure likes this green tea and aniseed mixes lately. I swear he even put King-of-bitters in one of them. Does he think he's funny? I don't think it's funny."

That was it.

"I'll get you some sweet tea. Eat your breakfast. That pastry made you grumpy," he mumbled to Mothy, walking right towards Haatji.

"See if they've got cat mint in theirs!" Mothy called out after him.

Wolflock made it to the distant table and leaned on the back of an empty chair. "Excuse me, ladies. Could I ask which tea is in your pitchers? Mothy doesn't like the bitter ones."

"I haven't tried them yet," Bleen yawned, shoving the silver jug towards him.

"I believe that is the sweet one," Haatji offered, keeping her gaze away from his.

Wolflock pretended to investigate the jug and scrutinize the liquid. "How did you fair after last night, Ms... Haatji?" As he spoke, he realised he didn't know her surname.

"I think I was as shaken as everyone else."

"Yes, but you actually had a proper altercation with Parihaan. Where did you go after the kitchen meeting?"

"When you had your head dunked in a barrel?" she sniffed.

Wolflock felt his face flush. He had never been so out of his own senses before, but he didn't think that his actions would be topical after the fact.

"I... Well... My investigation didn't go as smoothly as I'd have hoped but thank goodness for Grogen's miracle cure."

The twins chortled at his joke, but Haatji seemed too tired to even laugh. Her eyes were bloodshot, and the light olive skin around them was rubbed raw. Her brightly coloured niqab was wet around her cheeks where it soaked up her tears.

"Haatji came and stayed with us for most of the night. She needed to know where her future lay. She would have finished the reading if we hadn't been thrown into alarm by your discovery."

Wolflock looked at the twin that spoke, Bleen. Faleen and Bleen were identical twins who did all they could to avoid looking like the other. Bleen had violet coloured hair, which Wolflock assumed was natural, and it hung in luscious thick locks around her shoulders. She always wore layers of cool shaded fabrics, shawls, and clear or dark crystals on her rings, earrings, bracelets, and other clinking ornaments.

Her twin, Faleen, had dyed her hair bright orange, but the purple regrowth was starting to come through.

Unlike her sister, she cut her hair short and wore thick scarves around her head. All her clothing was in warm golds, yellows, oranges, and browns. She tended towards leather and wood carved trinkets and baubles for decoration.

The rumour on the ship was that Faleen was truly psychic, whereas Bleen was more observant.

"Oh?" Wolflock inquired politely, although he was unable to keep his tone from being a bit dry. "You looked quite startled when I came down to see you. Had you just received an unpleasant fortune?"

"To the contrary!" Bleen lifted her nose haughtily, "Our dear friend here was said to make a powerful ally and keep her secrets all where they should be kept."

Haatji's eyes went wide and shook her head a fraction to get Bleen to be quiet.

"Oh yes," the purple woman carried on as if she hadn't seen the queue. "She is to amass a fantastic fortune, be reunited with someone dear to her heart and regain the strength she-"

"We did each other's nails," Faleen cut in. Her voice was deep, low, and also raspy. "But Haatji, you've chewed yours off again. We'll have to do them up tonight."

Her unearthly voice gave Wolflock a chill, but it was better than Bleen's squawking. He glanced at Haatji's nails and saw a pretty copper paint had been chewed off and her nails were picked, jagged and cracked. She had an alibi. Wolflock felt his chest sink. He was sure she had known something more. But perhaps she did!

He reached into his pocket and pulled out Parihaan's book.

"Haatji? Does Uluken have many alphabets or writing styles?"

Her shoulders relaxed and she finally made eye contact with him. Her odd pastel green eyes were astonishing.

"There are different spoken languages between the desert tribes, but everyone knows Yumerias. It is the oldest trade language of Uluken. Why do you ask?"

"I found this, and I thought it looked like it was in an Uluken script. I was hoping I could get you to write me an alphabet out so I could translate it."

Haatji laughed, but it sounded like a hissing snake. "That is very cute, Mr Wolflock. It will take more than an alphabet or a dictionary to translate anything from Uluken. The language is more complex than Puinteylien."

"Oh. I see."

"Will you let me have a look at it? I could do with the distraction. I will translate it for you and write it back in Puinteylien for you. If it's written in an informal way it shouldn't be too difficult."

He hesitated, holding the book to his chest. "It... it may be sensitive information."

"I will be discreet."

Faleen and Bleen both watched them talking like a pair of hungry dogs.

"Perhaps not just yet."

Haatji smiled, her cheeks rising under her eyes. "I was about to go and do my prayers for the day, so if you would like me to translate it, I will be able to do so in the privacy of my own room."

She understood. Wolflock smiled, relieved. He handed her the little book and gave her a nod. At least there was someone on board who understood the delicacies of polite conversation. Myna would have loved her.

As he walked back to where Mothy was eating his third bowl of porridge, he felt a heavy pang in his gut. Visions of his little sister, his home, his horse, and the society he was used to flashed through his mind. He hated it, but he missed parts of it. Melancholy seeped into his posture as he waited for Mothy to finish his breakfast.

"You haven't eaten," he said through a mouthful of prunes and oats.

"I'm not hungry."

"That's... what? Two days? Three? Eat, Lockie."

"You're far too perceptive for your own good Myna- I mean Mothy. I... I'm going to go for a walk around the deck. I need a bit of fresh air."

Without waiting, Wolflock stood up and left the dining hall. He kept his word and walked around the deck, thinking. Haatji was definitely ruled out. If the twins could verify her alibi with them at the time when Parihaan fell and he could hear her chanting while the person with the knife came into the room, then it couldn't have been Haatji.

This left him with Geagle, Nan Ji, and Captain Blutro. Geagle was the next most likely suspect. He'd have to find and question him first. He couldn't seem to find the big blond dolt anywhere on the deck. He was meant to be entertaining the passengers soon. He always set up the worst games. Simple things and physical tasks that were too easy. Nothing that Wolflock found entertaining. Knowing he'd likely be late, Wolflock deduced that he'd be in the crew quarters finding the items for today's games.

He believed that his deck privileges would be restored enough that he could get away with going into the crew deck without severe repercussions. He descended below, only to find a few crew sleeping. Kolor, Hognut, Goden and Groger were all snoring in their hammocks.

No sign of Geagle though.

The sleeping crew members were still enough that Wolflock saw an opportunity. It wouldn't hurt now to check their shoes. The crew normally went about the ship barefoot as they said it gave them better grip and balance, but sometimes they would don shoes to go ashore or keep their feet warm. He could go around and sketch them down in his notebook. It would either find the culprit very quickly, or it would clear them all. He also might find Geagle's shoes and confirm his whereabouts last night.

One by one, Wolflock slunk between the hammocks and checked their shoe boxes bolted to the floor. The crew had three compartments each. A thin wardrobe attached to the wall, a side table with mirror and wash pan, and a long shoe box used for shorter crew to climb into their hammocks. None of them were locked except for a few of the bedside table drawers.

The hammocks caught Wolflock's attention though. He'd not given them much of a glance before and the crew quarters were always dim, so it was difficult to see. The hammocks were woven into a diamond pattern with little quilted pockets that made them look quite plush. Each diamond had little sigils and charms embroidered into them. Wolflock wondered if they were safety, sleep or good health, or a combination of many things. Each hammock was identical except for the varying pillows and blankets folded on them.

Looking through the crewmates' belongings gave him a new insight into each of them. Hognut had an extensive pipe cleaning kit, as well as a pristine silver beard trimming set. Grogen's only pair of shoes were lined with padded satin. Kolor had a small painting of herself from when she had long brown hair. Umkombe had a piece of wood as big as Wolflock's forearm that had glowing blue patterns across it. Malum, the second engineer had worn piano sheet music. Matroos, one of the Syongdelen crewmates, had hundreds of little ties for his thick long hair that he released into a spectacular afro on his rest days.

None of the shoes matched though.

Wolflock moved quickly between the last few beds, picking up Goden's shoes as he snorted in his sleep. The golden-ginger haired man wore a padded eye mask, and he had a bound stack of postcards from all kinds of places stored next to his single pair of simple brown lace up shoes. Wolflock lifted one and began sketching it. Nothing. Just a basic squared tread like most of the others. No floral designs.

Wolflock stood back up.

"What're doin', lad?" Goden tapped his shoulder.

Wolflock yelped and jumped, grinning sheepishly.

"Oh! Goden! You scared me!"

"Why'dya have my shoes? They won' fit ya, lad."

Thank goodness for the crew being slow.

"I was looking at the pattern. Veluse said I have a talent for sketching shoe patterns, and I wanted to get some inspiration!" Wolflock feigned a look of pride.

Goden groaned as he sat up in his hammock, setting his mask on his bedside table. He raised a sceptical eyebrow.

"You know I don' believe that, but I really don' care. Get upstairs and don' let me catch you down here again, lad. The crew need some kind of privacy from you lot."

Wolflock swallowed and backed away, understanding that he would be far less welcomed if he lingered. Irritated at the lack of clues, he decided to continue to wander around the deck until he found Geagle.

But first, he'd check in on Parihaan. He opened her door, hoping that it would be locked, and she would be safe, but it slid to the side with ease.

No one was here except for Parihaan.

She was sleeping on her bed in the exact same position. She looked so peaceful. In the late morning sun, he could see the little glints of tiny needles Nu had used to stimulate healing points.

Parihaan was alone though. He couldn't look for Geagle and leave her undefended. What if the knife person came back? Perhaps Geagle would come into the room to talk to her.

Wolflock entered, closed the door, and sat in the chair by the desk. The room was so still. He tried to let his mind wander, but the silence and the stillness made his thoughts jam. For a moment there was peace outside of him. It didn't last long. Wolflock crossed his long legs and uncrossed them. Leaned forward, leaned back. He rapped his fingers on the desk, picked his nails, and ran them through his hair.

Where was Nu?

"How are you, today?" he sighed, giving up on waiting in silence.

No answer.

"You know... I have a message for you. I was meant to give it to you last night, but I guess we all got a bit side tracked. You see... well... It feels silly to give it to you now. Listen, you'll just have to wake up. Then I'll tell you."

Wolflock sighed and leaned forward, resting his elbows on his knees, and intertwining his thin fingers.

"Who pushed you, Parihaan? I can see why they would have. You were quite irrational last night, and, when someone is not their full self, it can be awfully hard to connect to them. I just didn't think there was so much malice in any one person towards you. I also don't believe for a moment that you were the mastermind behind the alcohol smuggling.

"I found that note in your things. Who is A, Parihaan? I have so many questions. Where are you going? Why are you going there? Where did you come from? Why did you leave? Is it odd that I am more fascinated in your tale because you acted so strangely?"

He frowned as he rambled on to her. He was being silly. He didn't know what made him feel like he had to, but he reached out and gave her cool hand a little squeeze. He just hoped she felt it. "I just... I just wanted to tell you that you have friends."

Movement at the entrance of the room caught his eye. A large dark shadow flickered under the door.

"Hold that thought."

Wolflock rose and stepped to the side of the door, waiting for whoever was on the other side to open it. It slid open and Wolflock realised he couldn't let them into the room. It would be too late. They would be too close. He jumped in front of the intruder, blocking their way.

"AH!"

"Ahah!" He pointed triumphantly at Geagle. "I've been looking for you!"

It must have been something about Wolflock's excited demeanour that scared Geagle even more than usual. He clutched his breast pocket on his shirt as if he were protecting his heart.

"M-me?"

"Yes, you! Where were you last night when Parihaan fell down the stairs?"

"I-I-I was in the kitchen," he stammered.

"No, you weren't! I was in the kitchen and you were certainly not there. Try again. This time with the truth."

"I-It must have been just after you left then..."

"That still means that you could have been the one who watched Parihaan fall down those stairs." Wolflock smirked at his idiocy.

"I was in the-"

"And just one other thing before you try lying again. I know for certain that you were not on the top deck or within the sights of Haatji, Nu, or the twins, so don't try and tell me you were in the main crew hallway or with them."

Geagle gulped. "I think I- umm... You see..."

"I also know very well about your regular rendezvous with Parihaan and am quite curious as to why you thought you could do this when the Captain expressly forbids that level of fraternisation with passengers."

"But... He... I..."

"And you know that you're, how do you put it, *over a barrel*, with me knowing fully that you were instrumental in the smuggling of alcohol. You can't even plead plausible deniability since you were regularly dispensing it to Parihaan through the flask you gifted her."

"How did you... But... No, it's not..."

Wolflock waited with a broad smile. He'd caught him. Floral shoes or not, Geagle was hiding something and it was about to crack this whole case. The big man stepped back and gripped his chest harder, causing a crinkling sound.

"Captain told me that if you ask me things like this then I'm to tell you "Wolflock, stop!" and run away!"

And he did exactly that.

Geagle flew down into the crew area, leaving Wolflock perplexed, yet curious. What did he have in his breast pocket? And why was it so important that he had to protect it from Wolflock?

CHAPTER 5

A Lesson in Relieving

For once, Wolflock believed he had to consider how he was going to get the information he needed from Geagle.

He wouldn't have said that any of the crew were particularly intelligent. Knowledgeable enough in their own areas, but not apt at learning several languages, creatively solving problems, or putting pieces of evidence together. Geagle was even less intelligent than the others. Perhaps it was his youth or his mere lack of experience in life, but he was as thick as a sheep.

Initially, Wolflock didn't want to leave Parihaan

unguarded again, but he was relieved of his duty when Nu started coming down the stairs with more medicines, food and clean pins. She stopped and stared at him leaning at Parihaan's door again. Wolflock smiled and waved at her as he passed, to which she shrugged and carried on ahead from their unspoken understanding.

He pondered his next move in the midday sun, watching the stony banks lead up to sheer mountain peaks.

He wanted to pursue his lead on Geagle. It was the clearest one. He had the strongest motive, no known alibi, and he was strong enough to tête-à-tête with Parihaan. What had he gripped in his pocket though? Without that data, Wolflock couldn't hazard a guess. He huffed, hanging his arms over the ship's taffrail. Why had he revealed his whole hand to Geagle? He didn't have any new information over him that could be used to pry out the truth. And why had Captain Blutro told him what to say to him if he pressed for information? Had he confessed to the captain? Did the captain know more than he had let on?

Wolflock's head swam with thoughts he needed to catch.

Well, he did have one iron in the fire. He strode into the dining hall to find Haatji. He could smell seasoned vegetable and oat soup brewing for lunch, but no passengers had arrived yet. Turning about-face on his heel, he went to check her room.

He knocked on the closed door, and heard a quick scrape of her chair and a rattling before she spoke.

"Yes?"

"Miss Haatji?" He called through the door. "It's me. Wolflock. I was hoping to see if you'd made any progress on the book I gave you earlier?"

Silence hollowed the space between them for a few moments. Then he felt the door slide under his ear.

"I... I have gotten a few entries completed. They aren't my best work, but I'm sure they will suffice." Her voice was croaky, and her eyes were red again.

"Are you well, Miss Haatji?" He knew it was the polite thing to say, but more than that, he wanted to know why she was upset.

"I'm... I was... No. The diary is very hard to go through. I never knew she had lived such a hard life. Parihaan... well... this book has shown me a whole new side to her, and I feel wretched for lashing out at her the way I did."

"Don't worry, Miss Haatji. She's in good hands."

With a smile giving a slight rise to her cheeks, Haatji handed him a set of papers.

"They are in order. I will continue to translate them

if you like."

"Thank you. That would be appreciated." He took the pages and left her to her work.

Wolflock tucked himself away in his cabin and settled onto his bed, reading over the ten or so pages. The first entry was Parihaan's latest one, dated just before their stop at the Krieger Zwerg dock.

Lucimpus, 22nd of Eolas Revari, year eight of King Rayin

Everyone being excited about getting off the ship woke me up. I want to see what Geagle will buy me. This is meant to be a tourist shopping town. I hope they have sabaa' baharat. I'm so sick of the spices they use here. It's only salt and pepper most days. Geagle promised me he'd buy me all the spices I'd like. It was a bit over the top, but I think he's trying to make up for our argument. He's very sweet, but I know better than to trust a sweet man. Especially since I found his old love notes he promised he threw out.

I'd like to get back at him for upsetting me so much. I wish we didn't have to hide. He told me he'd ask the captain for permission, but he hasn't. I don't like the secrets. Keeping things hidden eats me up inside. Secrets are the devil's whispers into madness. He's confusing. I enjoy his company and I like his affection, but he has become so infatuated so quickly. It's a bit frightening. It's too much. But I feel guilty for liking it. Especially because of our fight with the letters. I wish he would write me letters.

Guilt keeps us aligned with the morals of the 'Bucde heilidrift', like any good person should follow.

Trost help me make the right choice.

Wolflock got a chill down his spine. Parihaan was a Troston. She followed the teachings of their principal book of scriptures. No wonder she spoke like she did the night she fell down the stairs. The Troston faith was less inclined to the practical and more inclined to self-depreciation in honour of their Lord. They were a newer religion in comparison to the local gods each city or town respected, and they believed that their single deity was the only real one and that they were omnipresent and vengeful. By living a life of pure selflessness that resulted in one's emaciation and injury, you would be permitted into a Skyland of eternal bliss. As Wolflock understood it, the more you suffered, the more you were rewarded in death.

It wasn't a common religion, and the membership was secular and small, but they stood out wherever they went because of their inharmonious beliefs. Trostons were the only people in all of Puinteyle who accepted slavery.

Wolflock thought back to Mothy. His best friend grew up in a farmstead and mill who were Troston. They had scarred his friend forever...

Wolflock set the pages down. Was he looking for a culprit who didn't deserve to be brought to justice? Had they done justice? What if Parihaan had owned slaves? Was he fighting for the wrong side? Should he stop? Could he stop?

He bit his lip and picked the papers up again.

Culimpus, 18th of Eolas Revari, year eight of King Rayin

I don't feel well. I don't like this foreign food. I miss home. I miss my bed. I miss everything. My faith is all I have left. What if I get sick and die? No one will care. I wonder if they'd even cry. My stomach feels so sore. Like I've eaten nails. Everything was going so much better. I had talked to the other people on the ship and I was even starting to look forward to seeing cousin Ithizaz. I haven't seen her since we were tiny, but she was the only one to reach out and help.

She is all I have. I hope she can help. I hope I can turn this corner.

I hope I survive.

May Trost give me strength.

Ahlwanye.

Sidumpus, 9th, Eolas Revari, year eight of King Rayin

Chelsii left two days ago. I am sad she was not on for longer. I will have to find someone new to talk to. The only person who came on is some young boy. At least we aren't locked in our cabins anymore. I didn't mind. It was bigger than my penance room, so I'm used to it. It has a window too and I could stare out of it for hours. The landscape is so green. Hanum (Haatji had written that the translation was roughly 'mother') *would be amazed to see it. She had only ever seen green along the river and in fabrics. I miss her most. If she had just been quiet. If she'd just ignored them and walked away, maybe we'd be able to make this trip together.*

At least I have her musihba. Sometimes I feel like

she is with me still.

Perhaps now that we are allowed to walk around, I may be able to finish my conversation with the handsome blond crewman. Chelsii gave me the confidence to at least try. I hope he talks to me first, so I don't have to.

Ahlwanye

Haatji had written a note underneath this entry saying that a musihba was a form of prayer beads passed down from mother to eldest daughter and that if Parihaan had her mother's beads, then she would have passed away.

Lucimpus, 23rd of Ha'ling Felst, year eight of King Rayin,

I was so close! I had everything ready and Chelsii said it would be a great idea. I had special serving cups and a nice new tray and everything. It's just my luck that I put the silly thing on the kitchen counter and then that stupid chef knocked it into the fire! I can't believe the crew can't handle the passengers out and about while the captain is ill. It's not fair!

It cost me ten deimas too...

At least I get to drink it while we're stuck in our cabins. I can't wait to get off this ship. Chelsii is the only friend I have and even she isn't so good. I told her the young blond crewman was attractive and she went and told him! I didn't mean it. I just wanted to spark up a bit of conversation with him.

I hope the bottle lasts me until we get to Creast.

Ahlwanye.

Lucimpus, 22n of Ha'ling Felst, year eight of King Rayin,

I'm going to try today. Chelsii said I should get a try and deliver just little drinks. We went shopping at the little stalls set up outside of Una (Some little town in Trost knows where), and I found a basic set of little cups and a wooden tray with a pretty design. Nothing like home, but it will do. I'm going to pour the drinks at dinner and pass them around. I think Chelsii wants more people to talk to us, and I wouldn't mind either.

I got the sweetest berry wine I could. Just like they did at church. Maybe they'll even let me say a prayer for them all too. I would like to talk to them all. I just feel so frightened of upsetting any of them. They all seem so nice. What if they hate me? What if I say something wrong?

No. I can't think like that. They're going to love the

drinks and we'll be good friends for it.
    Trost give me strength.

Ahlwanye.

As Wolflock looked through the rest of the pages, he wondered what had made Haatji cry. He couldn't find anything that was particularly moving or tragic, so he assumed she must have read through the rest of the journal first before she started translating. It was not a surprise to him that Parihaan hadn't signed off on the first entry he had read and the last entry she'd written. Someone must have approached her that very morning about helping them smuggle the drinking alcohol. The mysterious A, perhaps? He did have a new clue though.

Geagle had secret letters. Letters he still had in his possession after he and Parihaan began courting. He remembered Geagle had him write letters to previous lovers breaking off their relationships when Wolflock had been punished for causing a disturbance on the ship. His thoughts sprang back to Geagle holding his breast pocket. Wolflock had already been through his cabinets and cupboards, so the letters had to be on his person. He could wait for him to get changed and look through his clothes, but he wasn't able to get into the crew area anymore without raising suspicion. He also couldn't wait with Parihaan and keep an eye on Geagle at the same time.

If he got the letters, he might just have the evidence he needed to prove if Geagle has strong enough feelings towards Parihaan to push her down the stairs. Did he want to leave her? Had his feelings changed? Had Parihaan accused him of infidelity? Did he push her down the stairs so he could take up courting other ladies again?

Wolflock doubted that Geagle had a malicious bone in his body, but he couldn't rule it out until he had more evidence. He knew that the young blond crewman was the most indecisive person he'd ever met.

Nevertheless, he had to get some help. He was not an apt thief. But he knew someone who was.

It didn't take him long to find Mothy on the deck, smiling as he munched on an early lunch sandwich and watching the children play with a skipping rope. Wolflock smirked as he sat beside Mothy on the picnic blanket.

"So... I have a request," Wolflock started, coyly interlacing his fingers around his knee.

"Mmm?"

"That cake you took earlier..."

"Mmmm?"

"Would you show me how you did that?"

Mothy blinked, his mouth bursting with sandwich.

"Wffrr?"

"I don't speak fluent food."

He swallowed. "What for?"

"Well, I'm glad you didn't try and pretend you didn't steal them."

"We don't call it stealing." The straw haired boy waved his sandwich. "We call it relieving."

"I'd like you to teach me how to 'relieve' someone of something in their breast pocket."

Mothy laughed and finished the rest of his sandwich with surprising speed. "You've come to the right person, but you still haven't told me why."

"I believe there is a case afoot." Wolflock's eyes glittered with excitement as he started, but then he spotted the knife Mothy had brought out to butter his bread. The person with the triple edged blade was still out there. He couldn't endanger his friend like that. "I can't say what it is because I don't want to incriminate you just yet, but, as soon as I get the evidence I need, I'll tell you everything."

Mothy eyed him with his soft blue eyes, then shrugged and began buttering another sandwich. "Very well, but you need to tell me soon. It's so dull without you around, and Nu is so excited about her patient, I haven't seen her much either."

"Fantastic. How do we begin?"

"If you're to take something out of someone's breast pocket, there are a few things you need to know. We used to relieve the masters of keys, food, medicine and whatever we could get out of their pockets. Busy places are the best to get them. Lots of people bumping into each other makes things less obvious and people are distracted, meaning they won't look right away for the thing you take. Make sure they aren't paying attention to the area you're trying to grab at. If they're aware of it, you might lose a hand."

"Lose a hand?" Wolflock's eyes went wide.

"Perhaps not in normal society then... I haven't really done this kind of thing since back at the mill."

"Except for yesterday?"

"Except for yesterday."

"Why yesterday?"

Mothy blushed. "I... wanted to give Nu something special for her assignment and there wasn't anything I could make fast enough."

"Anyway, what do you look for next?"

"Someone with an easy target. Like a coin pouch or piece of loose jewellery sticking out. Then you bump into them. It's a common method apparently, so anyone with their wits about them will check their pockets and give chase if they catch on."

"Why use it then?"

"You only use it on dumb or distracted people."

"Any for harder targets?"

"No one is really a hard target. You just have to be adaptive. It's much easier when the target is around their waist or hips. Boots are harder to steal from. So are breast pockets."

"I thought we were calling it 'relieving'?" Wolflock smirked and elbowed Mothy's arm.

"Heh. Yeah."

"What about someone taller than you?"

"Then I hope you're good at running."

"That sounds like the attitude of a quitter, my friend."

Mothy chuckled and scoffed his second sandwich. He patted Wolflock's chest fondly before rocking back and forth until he was on his feet. "I think you need an example."

"Brilliant. Who are we starting on?" Wolflock felt a thrill of excitement run through him. Maybe Mothy would steal the letters for him.

"Well... you're going to have to get better at identifying when you've had something be relieved from your person." He flashed a wicked grin as he rolled Wolflock's pen between his fingers.

Flabbergasted, Wolflock patted his shirt and trouser pockets, thinking Mothy was joking and had a similar looking pen.

"How did you-?"

"You've got to be aware of yourself at all times. Distraction leaves you open." His friend laughed and pushed the pen back into his breast pocket. "If you can stop me from rifling through your pockets, I'll show you how to do the riffling."

Wolflock glanced back to the stairs leading down to the cabins. Surely, he'd see Nu come out and he'd be able to put a halt to their activities in time to keep Parihaan safe.

"Deal."

Mothy clapped his hands together. "Fantastic! I've wanted to chat with you all day. What did you think about the Captain's speech this morning?"

"I thought it was a bit premature to be honest. She isn't dead." Wolflock kept a keen eye on Mothy's left hand as he wrapped it around his shoulder, aiming for the pen again.

"I think some of the crew would say 'yet'." Mothy shrugged, twirling the rosewood handled magnifying glass Yifi had gifted him for Mabon.

Wolflock snatched back his magnifying glass and pocketed it again, pulling himself away from Mothy. He hadn't felt it move at all. "What did *you* think of his speech?" he glared.

Mothy shrugged and began refolding the handkerchief he'd taken from Wolflock's left trouser pocket. "I thought it was nice. I hope our prayers reach her, but I also hope she is a better passenger if she does wake up."

Wolflock took the handkerchief back, hyper aware of his three pockets. Mothy wouldn't get them again. "When. You mean when."

Mothy didn't come close again, but instead fiddled with something twinkling in his hands.

"You're very hopeful. It's not like you. Where is your sceptical nature gone?"

Wolflock realised he was attaching his insignia cufflinks to his tatty shirt. He saw something glint in Mothy's pocket. Mothy didn't own anything shiny. He had something in his pocket that wasn't his.

Wolflock unclipped his second cufflink and put it in Mothy's hand as he did up the first set. It looked so odd to see his glimmering silver cufflink on such a worn off white shirt. Twisting them into Mothy's cuff buttonhole, Wolflock popped the second one in and lifted Mothy's arms, turning his hands out to the sun so he could see them better. Seizing his opportunity, Wolflock gripped the sparkling metal object from his pocket.

"I think they look good on me," Mothy smiled contentedly.

"Now you just need this," Wolflock smirked as he nestled Nu's comb into Mothy's hair.

Mothy blushed and whipped the comb through his hair, hiding it in his palm. "I-"

"I won't ask why you have Nu's comb in your pocket." Wolflock raised his hands to call a truce.

"Good. Because, until you're ready to let me in on your new case, I'm not ready to let you in on my.... Nu.... case..."

Wolflock curled over laughing and Mothy shoved his head down, tussling his black hair.

"Sod off," he grumbled, folding his arms, but unable to keep his smile from the corners of his mouth.

"Oh, I knew there was a reason we were friends." Wolflock wiped a tear from his eyes and composed himself again. "Now, what if I wanted to get something from the breast pocket of someone who was taller than me and wasn't fond of me?"

Mothy snorted. "Who have you upset now?"

"It's less who have I upset and more who have I frightened."

"I'm not sure you realise how little that narrows it

down. Anyway. You've got to be able to distract them while you have the chance to touch the pocket you're trying to look through. If the pocket is tight, you'll need more time and a greater distraction. Normally getting into a scuffle with them works as long as they don't beat you to a pulp."

"Any other suggestions?"

Mothy put his hand in his pocket and looked up to his right as he thought. "Well... You can always pretend to fall out of the rigging onto them? If you did that, then they'd probably not notice you going through their pockets."

"How would I pretend to fall out of the rigging though?"

"Hmm... I guess you'd have to really fall out of the rigging."

"So, what you're saying, if I'm to get this correct, if I'm to pretend to fall out of the rigging, I'm to actually fall out of the rigging?"

"I feel like there is some kind of silly song happening here and I just can't quite put the words together. What rhymes with rigging?"

Wolflock chuckled, "Digging?

"Gigging. Wigging?"

"Are those even words?"

"They are now."

"I'll let you work on your new silly song while I find a way to pretend-for-real fall out of the rigging."

"And then you'll tell me what your new mystery is about?"

"If not then, soon after."

CHAPTER 6

Stealing Geagle's Heart

For some reason, since the ship had entered the windy mountain pass, Wolflock felt like the rigging looked rather precarious. Surely, there would be another way he could get into Geagle's pocket without having to first scale the wobbly ropes. The way they shook in the wind gave Wolflock all the excuse he needed to avoid getting above head height.

As the ship sailed through the mountains, a chilly breeze, laced with ice from the Shiriling tundra, began dancing across the deck. People stood closer together, they wore more clothing; even the crew had started wearing their shoes. None of which had a floral pattern on them, Wolflock noted.

He checked on Parihaan briefly before putting on his black jacket, then made his way to lunch, checking that everyone he suspected was there or otherwise engaged. Geagle oversaw the entertainment for the afternoon and decided that assaulting everyone's ears with his forlorn love poetry would be a good idea. For some reason, the older women in the company adored it, whereas everyone else seemed to politely applaud his efforts.

Wolflock did have to admit though, that, for a simpleton, he could spin a rudimentary poem as well as a half-trained bard. He never recited his poems from paper though, leading Wolflock to wonder if the youngest crewman kept them memorised or if he came up with them spontaneously.

At first, Wolflock applauded a little too loudly and approached Geagle at the end of the dining hall. He thought being enthusiastic for Geagle's performances would help to drop his guard, but instead it just left an awkward atmosphere.

"Top show, Mr Geagle. Absolutely charming. No wonder you're known on board as a ladies man," he tried to find a way to playfully tap his shirt pocket, but realised he was just a bit too far away and ended up producing an awkward hand movement between them.

"Thank you, Mr Wolflock, sir. I've been working

on those ones all week."

Ah, so he does memorise them.

"If you'll 'scuse me, sir. I have to get the deck games ready a'fore they finish dishes."

He nodded and Wolflock tried again to pat his chest in comradery, but Geagle put his hand to his heart and they clasped hands for a moment.

"Sorry!"

"Sorry!"

And with a beetroot red face, Geagle scurried off with his shoulders hunched.

Wolflock scrunched up his face in frustration and embarrassment. He had to look for another chance.

When lunch was finished everyone started drifting from the dining hall to try and spot mountain creatures or interesting rocks. There seemed to be all manner of trivia about the boulders strewn along the shoreline.

"We are entering one of the most historical parts of this river," Slavidus announced from the helm, the icy air whipping his salt and pepper ponytail behind him. "This was the best defended pass against the tyranny of the evil King Stathan. Refugees from his reign would come on the tiniest, shantiest boats as fast as they could. Women with children born during the ten-year massacre, magic users, witches, mixed nations people, and all manner of folk deemed 'irregular', flocked through this pass. This was the fastest way to escape, and, after the Krieger Zwerg tower was built, they were protected as soon as they passed it."

"How were they protected?" Tinni asked, taking her thumb out of her mouth to speak.

A small crowd had gathered around the helm stairs while Geagle hummed to himself as he set up the ring toss and charades cards.

"Each person who passed would leave an offering in the tower and be granted passage with a magical symbol. The Silver Ice Hair is blessed every single time we pass so we are protected on our journey."

"What did you give them?"

Wolflock's attention was focused solely on Geagle. Perhaps he could get the letters if he helped him set up... no... that wouldn't work...

The rigging gave an ominous shake, and he rolled his eyes. Not with this wind.

"Are you here to play the ring toss too, Mr Wolflock?"

"Huh?" He jerked his thoughts to who was addressing him. It was Didi, Nu's younger brother.

"I'm going to beat everyone."

The determination in his voice was nearly intimidating. He looked so serious about it.

"I'm sure you will," Wolflock patted the top of his head.

"I'm going to beat everyone." He whispered.

Backing away, Wolflock froze for a moment and caught a hint of inspiration. "You know what, Didi, I want to see you beat me at ring toss. Go on."

With a malicious glint, the tiny boy ran forward and collected his rings bound with four strips of blue ribbon.

Yifi, Tinni and Tanni joined in with the pink and yellow ones, and Wolflock grabbed the black ones. They were balsa wood painted silver, and were quite light. He flipped one ring in his hands while wearing the others as bangles. Mothy took up the red ones, eyeing Wolflock suspiciously, and Geagle stood back to adjudicate.

A knee-high maypole stood before them on a plank of heavy hardwood. The aim was simply to get as many of your rings onto the pole as you could. Wolflock normally preferred to analyse the trajectory and stratagem of the players, but he thought just for today he'd play. Especially if he could think of a way to get Didi to win. Then he could lift him up to give Geagle a celebratory hand gesture, or even better, throw him to Geagle in celebration. Geagle would be distracted and, when he went to take the child back from him, he could slip the letters out of his pocket.

Yes. It was a good plan.

They started their game and Wolflock realised he forgot to factor in the fact that Didi was terrible at this game. Every time he got close to the maypole he would change his style dramatically and miss. Wolflock even called for there to be a height ratio that let them stand closer if they were shorter, but Didi threw a tantrum.

Tinni, on the other hand, was a great shot.

With a shrug as she won the last round, Wolflock hoisted her up. She squealed with delight and with a one, and a two, and a three, he launched her to Geagle and stepped forward.

He hadn't expected Geagle to toss her right back at him. The little broad faced girl flew back at Wolflock, but he had already walked forward, making the throw misjudged. Tinni smashed into his chest and they both fell to the ground. Tinni kept laughing as if it was the best time in the world, but Wolflock's back ached from the fall.

"Sorry there, Mr Wolflock sir! I thought you'd catch her good!"

Wolflock sat up and gripped his black hair, scrunching his face until the pain dissipated. "I'm fine," he wheezed. "I'm fine."

He thought for a moment Geagle might come and help him to his feet, but Yifi grabbed him by the arm, Tinni hanging around his neck like a maramuti, and brought him upright.

He noticed that she still looked as stunning as ever. Slavidus hadn't given her the enchanted gemstone yet…

"You're such a good big brother." She smiled with a disarming beauty.

"Hah. Tell my little sister that," he sighed, watching Geagle pick up the rings and reset them.

"I did not know you had a sister, Lockie."

Nu's soft voice gripped his full attention. She was up here for lunch. That meant Parihaan was unguarded. He didn't have time for more games.

"I'm going to have a stroll. My head got a bit more rattled than I first thought." Mothy's full attention was on Nu and Yifi's attention was on listening to Tinni, giving him the chance to sneak off. To his horror, he could see Geagle doing the same thing, letting Didi run the ring toss for him.

This was it then.

The rigging shook in the wind as a new gust taunted him. There was just something about deliberately putting oneself in actual danger that made him reluctant. Partly because the rigging had made him nervous since he had been tangled in it during one of his and Mothy's ventures.

He also didn't like the idea of intentionally throwing himself onto someone. He could get hurt. A lot.

But Parihaan could die.

He swallowed his fear and his piercing blue eyes darted around. He judged the distance, size and velocity needed to take care of the task. He saw Geagle just a few yards from the entrance to the passenger cabins. Without another thought he dashed to the rope ladders and gripped it tight. He barely noticed Hognut tapping his pipe out right beside him.

"What in Houl's name are yeh doin'?" he grunted as Wolflock swung around and started climbing.

"I'm trying to land on Geagle so I can check his pockets for evidence," Wolflock said rapidly as he clambered up the cords.

"O' course yah are..." Hognut sighed, tapped his pipe and walked away.

Wolflock scaled the rigging, his knuckles turning white whenever the slightest breeze made the ropes tremble. He crawled across the beam at the bottom of the sails, thankful that the wind only pushed him into the sails and not off the twelve-foot-high structure.

Geagle was at the entrance to the deck below. He was too late.

Wolflock gritted his teeth and tensed. He had one chance still. He couldn't give up. Like a released spring, he sprang from the beam and prayed to the wind that he'd be carried far enough. He regretted it immediately.

Wolflock and Geagle tumbled down the stairs into a painful heap. Not only had hitting Geagle in the back hurt, but so had hitting every stair on the way down and splatting on the ground like a bucket of water.

"Ouch! What on- Mr Wolflock?"

Groaning, Wolflock rolled over coughing, holding his stomach from where Geagle's elbow had caught him. Worst of all, Geagle seemed like he was completely fine.

"Are you hurt? What happened?"

Wolflock coughed, gripping his lower ribs, "I'm fine. I'm fine. I slipped."

Geagle pulled his hands away quickly and took a step back as if he'd been zapped. He stiffened, his shoulders high and his face flushed red.

"What?" Wolflock felt as if everything creaked as he moved.

"Nothing." The crewman squeaked. "Merry part."

As Geagle left and went down to the crew quarters, Wolflock grinned. He had the letters from Geagle's pocket tucked between his stomach and hand. The ache in his ribs was worth it.

A Study in Silver

CHAPTER 7

The Most Foolish Poet

Wolflock grinned to himself as he entered his room. He'd find out the truth now. He'd find out what Geagle had been writing and why it would lead to him pushing Parihaan down the stairs.

His hand touched the silver lever on his door, but he stopped. Geagle may have gone downstairs, but he could always come back up. Nu was at lunch.

With a sigh, he let his hand drop from his own door and he moved to Parihaan's. He had to keep watch. Maybe she'd wake up as he read through the letters. Wouldn't that be a shock for her? At least his face would be a friendly one.

The room was still except for the breeze coming through the window, rustling the curtain and the herbs Nu had strung up over Parihaan's bedhead. It was different though. It felt cleaner. On the edge of the wastebin was a grubby rag, soaked with oil. Clove. Nu had purified the room. The strong odour was enough to sting his eyes after a few minutes, so he pushed the porthole window open more.

"You're not missing out on too much," he said absentmindedly, staring at the cliffs to the port side. "Just rocks for now. Apparently, they have historical significance. Do you find that kind of thing fascinating? I don't unless it has some effect on the immediate vicinity or situation. You know? Suppose those rocks marked out a path that could be traversed for hidden ingredients used in a specific potion. Or if they were a significant hiding spot for thieves who had stolen a magical goat. That's what would interest me. Judging by your notes, I think you'll like to know if there was a romantic story behind them that had enthralled your friends."

He looked back at her as if she were about to respond. She kept laying there. Yellow eyes closed. Black hair braided over her shoulder. Hands folded on her stomach. Barely moving with her breath. His heart sank with disappointment.

His chest heaved with a sigh and he sat down at her desk. He flicked Geagle's letters open and rested his cheek in his hand as he read them. Geagle's handwriting was atrocious. The crooked, savagely indented letters were barely legible, and the odd loops sometimes dwarfed their stems, and other times looked like tiny smudges. Several of the scraps of paper were just the common Puinteylien alphabet written over and over.

Dear Ji'enna,

I will always remember how your hair shines like the darkest sun and I long for your warmth once again. Write to me soon.

Love, Geagle.

Dear Teast,

I miss your giggle like the brooks miss the cool dusk that reminds them they don't always have to beat back the day.

Love, Geagle.

Dear Shorgalen

My heart beats to the words you wove for me as if it is the song of my love for you. I am only half a man every

moment we are apart.
Love, Geagle.

Wolflock wanted to gag. Such saccharine nonsense and for what? Women he'd never see again? Women who probably didn't know about each other. It all sounded ridiculous.

He examined the paper closely with his magnifying glass to find the edges were worn and the ink looked fairly old. He wished he had the means to properly identify the date and in which location they were written. He'd be able to tell if they were written before or after Parihaan's fall. They seemed old, but how old? Were these the letters Parihaan was upset about in her diary entry?

As Wolflock flicked through twelve different love letters, he came across an open envelope with several short notes attached to it. Geagle had written a few noticeably short letters to this one. Why was this so special?

Dear Deanya,
I can't accept your gift. Please send me a return address so I know where to send it back to.
Love, Geagle.

Dear Deayna,

I don't know when the ship will come back to Corl. Do not wait for me. I will write this too slow to catch you. Go to the ball without me.

Love, Geagle.

Dear Deayna,

I don't know who you are talking about. I didn't see anyone on the ship who looked like that. Please stop writing.

Love, Geagle.

Dear Deanya,

Please don't cry but I don't want to write to you anymore. I am not in love with another woman, but you are scary.

Love, Geagle.

Wolflock frowned. Geagle was trying to reject a woman's advances? From the letters he'd written for the crewman before the Tuiti fruit incident, and his propensity to declare his undying love at the slightest whim, he couldn't understand why. What made this woman different? Was he really frightened of her? Was she his new fling just before he met Parihaan? Had she encouraged him to do away with Parihaan? Why did he sign them all with "Love"?

The attached pink envelope was decorated with elaborate swirling flowers and hearts, and across the front in silver ink was Geagle's name. Silver ink? This could be the evidence he needed to show that he had been present when Parihaan had fallen. Wolflock turned the envelope upside down; a sickly smelling letter and a lock of hair fell out. It smelt like a terrible raspberry cough medicine mixed with honey.

The lock of hair was a distinct auburn with red streaks, tied with a dainty pink bow. Dainty was definitely the word to describe the entire package. The writing was prim and neat, the envelope was sealed with bright pink lipstick marks, and the folded letter that fell out was of matching stationary. Only Geagle's name was written in silver throughout the letter. The rest was in normal black ink.

To my dearest, most darling Geagle,

I count the hours since we last laid eyes upon each other. The wind sings your name to me and I often stand by the pier watching the water, expecting to see your shimmering ship sail back to my heart. I have your lock of hair, and I thought you should have another of mine. So sweetly do I cradle your luscious strands. Every waking moment of my life is filled with longing for you. I only eat the foods I could dream of eating from your fork. I drink only from a goblet I have imagined you giving to me. Father says I must let you go, but our destined love will rejoin us once more.

Every song I hear at the opera I picture you singing to me. I long so deeply to be one of those ladies swooning in your arms. I only dress in your favourite shade of turquoise. It still makes me laugh to think you called it "wet green". How delightfully insightful you are. Such wit. Such mental prowess. I know that, when you give up sailing for me and marry me here, you will make a fine scholar.

I know you'll always be true to me, and I love that you are so honourable. Mother has shown me more spells to cast to help me see you in our dreams. I can nearly project my visage as far as the Syongdelen border. Let me know when you see me, especially if it's before I see you, my darling river knight. When my friends tell me you will have a woman in every port, I rebuke them. I tell them that my Geagle's heart is mine and mine alone. I tell them of the promises you made me and how you are ever honest and faithful. They tell me I'm a fool and I promise that, if they say it once more, we shan't be friends anymore.

My days are so dull without you, but I hope that if I

relay my trite motions you shall inject them with a light as golden as your mane...

Wolflock felt as if he became less intelligent the further he read. Six pages of her drivel and pining. She never mentioned where she lived, but, from her in depth descriptions, he could glean that she lived in Corl. He wondered if she knew his cousins. He was sure, from the encounters he'd had with them, that they would have been capricious friends together.

If Parihaan had found this, or even caught a glimpse of it, it could have been enough to make her confront him. Did he push her to get rid of the drama? Emotional motives could lead to the most spontaneous results and dire consequences.

Wolflock had suffered from that a few times. When he had justly called out the secretive actions of the upper echelon of Plugh, he had been verbally and physically assaulted. Once, after outsmarting the Thorn brothers, which was no hard feat, they had caught him, gut punched him, stripped him naked and left him to walk home through the city. Luckily for him, it had rained recently, so he fashioned himself garments of mud and sticks to protect his modesty.

It hadn't worked. He hated that city.

Folding up the letters again, Wolflock smiled to himself.

"I'd best go and return these to Geagle. I doubt you'd like to see them, but I would recommend courting a gentleman who can make up his mind as to which partner he'd like to pursue. Discussions on monogamy and fidelity are always important to establish straight away, I do believe."

He patted her hand again and stood by the door, stretching his legs until Nu arrived to replace him.

"We are taking shifts?" she raised her thin black eyebrow.

"Indeed."

"I shall leave medicine and instructions for you next time. You will be my intern," Nu smirked.

"I think Mothy would be a far better intern. I'm just the watchman."

They traded places and Wolflock went to find Geagle. The passengers were performing book recitals with dramatic hand gestures and voices. Wolflock spied his suspect walking around the crowd, searching the ground with a red face.

"Looking for something?" Wolflock sneered, holding the letters between his index and middle fingers.

"Huh? How did you- Those aren't yours!"

"Indubitably."

"Give them back!"

"Only after you tell me why Parihaan was so emotional with you the night she fell down the stairs." Wolflock held the letters behind his back as Geagle snatched for them.

"I dunno! She just was!"

"Well, I guess Ji'enna doesn't need to know how dark her hair shines."

Geagle's face paled. "You read them?"

"It's not like they took long to get through. I wonder what the Captain will think if he finds out you've been so frequently fraternising with passengers."

Wolflock made eye contact with Geagle. His sharp blue eyes locked with the droopy ones of the bulky crewmate before him. Something snapped behind those pitiful eyes. Wolflock saw the twitch in his eyebrow. He saw the pupils shrink. He knew he was in danger.

Geagle's eyes flickered between Wolflock's face and the letters being twirled through his long fingers. He brought his elbow back. He was about to charge.

Wolflock took off like a fox. He had to find a place to hide. Geagle wasn't going to speak. His job and his freedom were on the line. As he rounded the front mast, he glanced back to see how much distance he'd gained, but

Geagle was young, fit, and leaner than the other crewmates. His hand caught a few strands of Wolflock's hair and the teenager yelped, slid under his high grasp and shot forward.

A plan flashed through his mind. Climb the rigging, get to the crow's nest, leap into the sail, escape down through the Captain's balcony and hide in the tunnel. Geagle would have time to cool off and he'd be safe. He just had to get enough distance to get a head start on the rigging.

His heart pounded against his ribs as he vaulted over a pair of barrels and changed direction away from the dining hall. He leaped over Nan Ji and Stra on the deck, who scoffed, then shouted as Geagle vaulted them too. He could feel Geagle hot on his heels. He just couldn't get away. It was worse, too, that every now and then Wolflock felt a tug at his jacket. Geagle was so much faster than the other crew members.

Skipping his first three steps, Wolflock raced around the dining hall, sliding around the corner as he went. He'd just have to make a jump for the Captain's balcony and pray that the wind would keep him safe. He gripped the taffrail and hoisted himself over the edge. Then he came to a jerking halt.

His jacket pulled tight and his shirt caught him

around the throat.

Geagle slowly lifted him up, not even panting. Wolflock had neglected to calculate just how athletic the young man was.

"Give. Them. Back!"

As he slowly revolved around, he realised he'd never seen Geagle look so furious.

"Not until you tell me what you were doing when Parihaan was pushed down the stairs!" Wolflock glared at him, gripping his thick wrist with one hand, and holding the letters behind him at the same time.

Geagle looked around, obviously not thinking of a response to the question. Holding the dark-haired boy over the railing, he walked along the edge and held him over the water.

"Give them back or I'll drop you."

Wolflock saw the rushing blue water beneath and lost his words. It would be cold. Maybe freezing. He'd have to swim, fully clothed, to the edge of the water and walk back to the nearest town, which was over a fortnight away. He'd die of starvation or animal attack before he was ever found again.

"Listen." He tucked his legs up and tried to reach the taffrail, but Geagle had him at a rather inconvenient angle. "Listen. I understand. You loved Parihaan. You wanted to help her. I saw you both. You were trying to do your best for her. You can't help who you fall in love with. If you throw me off now then you'll have to make the choice of how you're going to tell the Captain and Mothy why I'm missing, or if you're going to lie. Then you also never get to send your lovers their letters. You'll lose the proof of Deanya's obsession. Everyone will just think you didn't care about her and she'll always be able to excuse the help she clearly needs."

Geagle's face scrunched up with difficult thoughts as Wolflock spoke, but the fury remained tumultuous behind his eyes. "You're lying. You don't know anything. You're making it up."

He shook Wolflock and his eyes narrowed.

"Why would I be making it up?" He fumbled trying to put the letters in his pocket deep enough that they wouldn't fall out.

"Because you're jealous," Geagle growled.

"Jealous? What? How on Pelaia did you come to that conclusion?"

"You've been trying to get close to me all day. You were in Pari-rose's room waiting for me. You told me you'd been watching me, and you know about my meeting with her. That's what Deanya used to do. You complimented me so much on my poetry that even Miss Yifi said it was odd. You touched my hand deliberately!"

Wolflock felt his face get hot. He'd been so obvious that even this dullard could tell what he was up to!

"You played ring toss when I ran it. You never play ring toss! Then you were spying on me and fell out of the rigging. You only stole those letters to get close to me now that Parihaan is out of the picture."

Wolflock kept his mouth shut and just stared. Where was Geagle going with this?

"I'm sorry, Mr Wolflock, but I'm just not interested. But you have to give me back my letters."

His piercing blue eyes darted left and right, then back to Geagle. Did he think he was romantically interested in him? He needed the information about where the crewman was last night.

"Well..." Wolflock said slowly, thinking as quick as he could, "I'm sorry for my actions." He couldn't play the truth card of him just looking out for Parihaan and trying to give her justice because, if Geagle was the attempted murderer, then he'd surely throw him off. But if he thought Wolflock was after Parihaan's heart he might get jealous. As he dangled there over the edge of the ship, he realised that he was dealing with less of a passive imbecile, and more of a dangerous bull. "You've clearly thought this through quite thoroughly, but I think you need to decide on something more important."

Was he going to throw him off the edge of the ship if he returned the letters anyway? He didn't want to remind him of why he had Wolflock dangling over the edge of the ship, but he had to get answers.

"What's that?"

"Firstly, it's not accurate that I am interested in you more than being acquaintances," Geagle's face relaxed, but after a moment he frowned in confusion. "Secondly, have you decided to send your letters separating from Deanya? Or are you going to marry her so none of your future relationships get pushed down the stairs?"

Geagle grimaced, "You don't know what you're talking about."

Wolflock knew he'd hit the nail on the head as he saw Geagle's thick arm slacken slightly.

"She's been using magic on you. You can't even hide from her in your dreams. Soon she'll be able to project herself onto the ship and haunt you always. You won't be able to see any other women."

He thrust Wolflock out further.

"Or not! Not if you decide to banish her from your life! All I want to know is; did you push Parihaan down the stairs to save her from Deanya's wrath? Or was it to allow you to pursue the other ladies in your pocket?"

The turmoil crossing Geagle's soft features was excruciating. "Stop!"

"It's a big decision, yes? A noble decision, even! I-I can help you make it. No one here can see that like you can. I bet they make fun of you for it. You've got so many choices. What do you think is the correct one?"

His arm slackened again.

"You've got to choose between your work on the ship, which I know you love. All these friends, the Captain, the travel, the lifestyle. You love it. Then you have to choose between the love of all these women you've met. It's, what, six?"

"Twelve," Geagle sighed, his arm lowering even more, allowing Wolflock to get a foot on the edge of the ship.

"Twelve! That's huge! So many hearts. I bet you would love to have them all, but they think they're being monogamous, yes?"

"Some do..."

"Exactly. It must be so hard keeping track of them and making sure you have the best poems and gifts to send them," Wolflock waved his arm out to try and grab the railing, but could only flail. "Then you have dear Parihaan-rose -Pari-rose - unconscious downstairs, right beneath our feet. Her spirit is probably crying out for help right now.

She's wondering why you're in this situation and not helping me help her."

Geagle's arm dropped enough for Wolflock to graze the grey railing, but not quite catch it.

"Then you have to decide what to do about Deanya. She's impacted all of your other lovers and your ability to focus on them. She's tormenting you. She's so hard to get rid of though, correct? You don't want to upset her but she's upsetting you."

Geagle let go of Wolflock as he brought him to the railing, then slumped against a crate, all anger replaced with despair.

"What do I do, Mr Wolflock, sir?"

Wolflock scrambled onto the deck on all fours, clutching his heart. His ears were pounding from his racing blood and he felt like he was going to faint.

That was the first time I've ever been let go. Mothy is helping me to be very convincing!

"Where," he panted, not ready to be higher than a knee yet, "were you last night?"

"How will that help?"

"You're going to have to trust me." He looked up at the crewman, trying to stop the contempt from creeping across his features. "I'll be able to help you if I have all the information."

"I-"

Something made a noise just beyond the dining hall corner. Like someone putting a metal container on a barrel. Both of them stopped, looking up and holding the silence. Was someone listening to their conversation?

"I feel like I should show you. It's easier." Geagle's cheeks had gone pink again. "I didn't want the other crew to know. They might tell the Captain or Slavidus and I'd get in trouble."

Wolflock shrugged and they walked along the deck, drawing the surprised glances of the company waiting to see if Geagle would still chase him around the mid deck. Geagle glanced around as they moved into the passenger cabin deck, but instead of proceeding to the crew deck, Geagle turned into Ungul and Uhnha's old room.

It had been empty for a week and, to Wolflock's knowledge, only the crew had come to clean it and keep it fresh until they picked up other passengers from future docks. Geagle slid the door open and began rifling through the desk draw.

Wolflock stood by the door watching him. The room still had a tinge of Syongdelen leather scent in the air. The two bunks were stripped of bedding and the curtain was drawn across the porthole window.

"I was in here. I was meant to be in the crow's nest,

but I was so upset that I came here. I always use the empty rooms for my writing."

Geagle pulled out a thick wad of scrap paper covered in scribbles and scratches. At a glance, Wolflock could see the top page was poetry.

"I felt embarrassed that we used so much paper to write my letters that you helped with before everyone got sick with the river bugs, so I thought I'd practice my own writing so I could get good, ya see?"

"Indeed," Wolflock said slowly and picked up a loose piece torn from the brown paper used to wrap leftovers in the kitchen.

I need your love to keep me warm Like the fires burning inside of us, pushing us over the edge of insanity, keeping us so close together in heart and, yet, so far apart in miles

Wolflock's nose wrinkled in distaste.

"Here it is! This is the one I was working on when Parihaan was found."

Geagle thrust a page from Slavidus' logbook into Wolflock's hands. It had a significant amount of scribbles.

To my rose, let me sooth your pain, let me end your

woes. You may beat my chest and bite my toes. You can never hurt me through my shield of love. I will be here for you always and forever. We will work through this together...

It was a rather lengthy letter with several sections crossed out and rewritten.

"How quickly can you write?" Wolflock asked, feeling the threads of his case beginning to detach themselves from Geagle being the culprit.

"I'm getting better." He smiled with enthusiasm and snatched up a pencil, writing on the back of one of the scraps of paper. "See?"

Wolflock watched him painstakingly write his name along with the sentence "can't choose who his heart desires". It took several minutes. If it took him this long to write a single sentence, yet he wrote half a page last night, he wouldn't have had the time between the altercation and Wolflock finding Parihaan to have pushed her down the stairs.

"Does this help?"

Wolflock sighed. "Yes. Unfortunately. You kept thinking you could make amends with her, didn't you?"

Geagle nodded, his eyes desperate for the solution Wolflock had no interest in giving.

This wasn't his culprit. He had been tucked away in here. The back of the paper still had a date at the top from where Slavidus had started using it and made enough mistakes to tear it out. He remembered seeing the light on under the door last night. His alibi was very well near verified. Near enough at this stage.

"So, what should I choose?"

Wolflock put his stupid love poetry on the desk and rolled his eyes. "Honesty is always the best policy. Even if it hurts. If you don't want to choose a single partner, you need to tell them you don't want to. They have the informed choice on if they want to choose you or not. As for Deanya, tell her the truth. Tell her you're uncomfortable. Tell her you don't think you're right for each other and that you have moved on. And, for the Captain and your career, explain your true nature to him and tell him you can't help yourself. Deceiving these people causes both parties pain in the long term. Honesty causes pain in the short term, but at least it allows for growth. You have to have the courage to be honest and give people the chance to choose you."

Geagle's eyes welled up with tears and he gazed thoughtfully at the ground. "That was beautiful. I need to write that down! That's the perfect break up poem for Deanya!"

Wolflock raised his eyebrow as the young crewman took up his pencil and began writing at his speedy snail's pace. As he left the room and contemplated his own words. He had to be honest. And, at this stage, he had to consider one of the people he didn't want to consider for the sake of his friendship with Mothy and Nu.

He had to consider that the only real suspect left was Nan Ji.

122

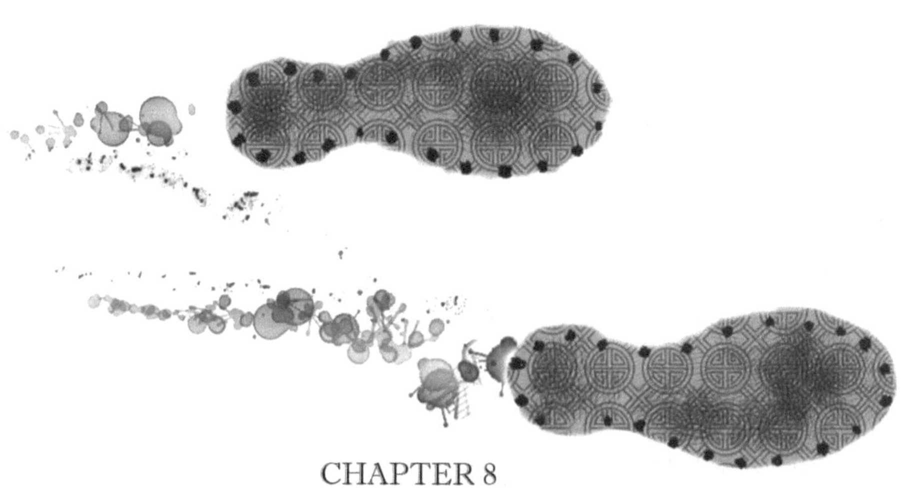

CHAPTER 8

Bad Bedside Manners

"Ceagle? May I ask something of you?" Wolflock eyed the hallway, thinking of how he wanted to start investigating Nan Ji, but also make sure Parihaan was safe.

"Hmm?"

"Nu and I have taken turns to make sure Parihaan has assistance at all times just in case she wakes up. Would you mind helping us with our shifts?"

"Of course, Mr Wolflock, sir. I will never leave her unattended. She will have a happy face to wake up to as soon as she's able."

"Good man. Perhaps you can write your poetry

beside her and keep her company."

"That's a great idea!"

Wolflock smiled politely as he saw the lovestruck fool take up his pen and letters and move into the room down the hall. At least there was one more set of eyes keeping track of her. Between the three of them, surely the person with the knife wouldn't dare strike again. He saw the Nan family's room closed. Was anyone napping in there? Were they all on the deck? He knew Nu was in the dining hall getting lunch and Nan Ji was socialising. Gege and Didi shouldn't be too far from his side. He might just have a bit of time to check their shoes for the right prints.

Seeing no one was in the hallway, he slipped through the unlocked door and closed it behind him. The Nan family's room smelled like their medicinal potions and Xiayahn cleansing products. Acrid, yet cloying.

Everything else about the room was pristine. All the clothes were folded into tight squares, all the shoes were laid out in perfect order. The four bunk beds were made as if someone had checked them with a ruler, and nothing was left out at all.

Each bed had a travelling trunk with scuffed gold designs of landscapes and dragons. The bottom two beds had their trunks on the floor, but the top two had a shelf at the foot of them for a storage space.

It was the shoes he was after, though. He could easily guess which shoes belonged to each person by size, but what he found inside them was curious. Nu's shoes were empty, as were Nan Ji's, but Gege's shoes had a hand drawn sketch of the mountain pass. Didi had hidden a toy soldier in his shoe. None of them had a floral pattern.

What if he had more shoes in his trunk? Wolflock had to know.

He knew Nan Ji slept on the bottom left bed, so he flicked open the trunk with a click. Inside, Nan Ji's clothing sat neatly folded on top with a side compartment for papers in his native language. He carefully pulled out the clothing and sat it on the bed, keeping it tidy. At the bottom he found two pairs of shoes made of fine cloth. Embroidered with the most delicate images of various plants growing along them, they were the right size, but, as Wolflock turned them over, he found that they had no nails. Apparently shoes from Xiayah were stitched.

He huffed, thinking he'd found another dead end, but then saw that the intricate design of the soles had little dots that could make the same marks in the dust as nails. Neither of these beautiful sets of shoes had a pattern that matched the set he'd copied the prints from. That meant that, if Nan Ji was the suspect, he would be wearing the same shoes at that very moment.

Heavy footsteps creaked on the stairs right outside the room, reminding him to speed up his search. Wolflock put the items back the way he found them and quietly closed the case. He pressed his ear to the door, careful not to make it bump against the frame. He'd wait for these people to pass and then slip out, but, if Nan Ji or one of his children came down first, he'd jump in the closet to hide.

"Captain," Slavidus called out, "Captain, wait!"

"I don't want to hear it, Slavidus. She was trouble from the start. We're all better off leaving things as they are."

"But sir, what if it was sinister? You can't tell me, when you left the wheel to Canhop last night, that you didn't see anything. There are clear signs someone else was down there with her and didn't report it-"

"Enough!" barked Captain Blutro. "I have said enough. Veluse has been in my ear all afternoon about it. She is in better hands now she's not on her own. I wish we had a closer port to get her medical attention, but we don't, so we have to trust that young girl is sufficient."

"Captain," Slavidus' tone softened. "I know it's been a hard few days. I know she was hard to handle at the best of times, and, after what you said about the smuggling-"

"Slavidus, I'll not hear another word about this.

What's done is done. I don't want anyone on the ship discussing this or the smuggling. If I hear even a peep..." The Captain sounded dejected.

"I'm sorry, sir. I just knew I saw blood on her nails, and I was frightened that an actual crime had taken place."

"I say there hasn't been one."

"And so there hasn't been one."

"Thank you. I just want this issue to be over. It's brought up enough old wounds as it is."

"I understand, sir. I'll quell any rumours that surface."

As the sound of the Captain's footsteps dispersed, Wolflock admired Slavidus' diplomatic approach and reasoning. The first mate was smarter than he had originally given him credit for. Slavidus was standing right outside the door still, though. Someone humming trotted down the stairs.

"Ah! Pardon me, First Mate," Veluse chuckled as he slid his own door open a few down from the Nan Family. "I was wondering if I could possibly have some lanterns brought on the deck for light so I could paint the beautiful sky over the mountains."

Slavidus sighed. "Not tonight Veluse. Also, you'll find that nights in the pass are particularly black."

"Ah, such a pity," Veluse seemed undeterred by his

tone. "I shall have to imagine it then."

Slavidus had a lighter step than the captain, but Wolflock could still hear him leave. He slid the door open and closed it behind him. The ship was in shadow from the sun having dipped beyond the mountains and the chill of the air had grown. He'd have to go and find Nan Ji's shoes or wait until he went to sleep.

He decided to walk about the deck and see if he could spy Nan Ji's shoes. But, between the shadow of the mountains and his proper posture, Wolflock couldn't even get close to catching a glimpse. It didn't help that he was one of Nan Ji's least favourite people onboard and it was obviously suspicious when he approached.

Eventually he had to concede the evening's defeat. Geagle was absent, so Wolflock took that as his opportunity to relax and eat. He hadn't realised how hungry he was until he smelt the delicious roast vegetables and spiced duck. The brightness of the dining hall gave him an idea. Perhaps he could get Nan Ji's shoeprint after all...

"Lockie! You're here! We've been talking about our studies. What do you think you'll study at Mystentine? Nü, would you please pass the cranberry sauce?"

Wolflock sat down and collected a drumstick and roast vegetables. They were cooked so perfectly that the thin skin had a beautiful crispiness to it, yet the inside was still juicy.

"I'd like to study the human mind, social patterns and the subtle details of crime so I can solve cases faster and more accurately than the Guard can..." Wolflock trailed off as Nü reached over. Her sleeves pulled backup to her elbows to show perfect porcelain skin. It was flawless and looked as if it was made of satin. There were no scratches. Parihaan had drawn blood from whoever pushed her. There should be deep marks on whoever was present when she fell. With that evidence, her thread in Wolflock's mental web came to the conclusion that she was innocent.

The shoe print, the scratches, and the silver. Those pieces had to go together.

"What of you, Mothy?" Nü asked with a warm smile.

"I'm not sure yet. I'd like to help people though."

Wolflock watched Nan Ji; his arms were covered up to his hands. He'd been infuriated with Parihaan, but was it enough to kill? He knew Nan Ji and Parihaan had pushed him to fury. Had she done this again and incurred his anger in the hull? Where had the silver come from and how could Nan Ji have access to it?

"You could study to be a doctor." She shrugged. "I

think you would make a very good doctor. You are good with people. Very gentle."

Mothy blushed bright pink and fumbled the sauce as he took it from Nü.

"Oh, I'm not clever enough to do medicine..."

Wolflock was plucked from his thoughts by Mothy's words. "What are you talking about?"

"Well, to be in medicine, you have to be really book smart. You have to study heaps and then you have to remember all the procedures, the surgeries, the medicines, the combinations and everything."

Wolflock and Nu looked at each other with mutual astonishment.

"I never even went to school. How could I become a doctor?"

"I went to school for a month before I refused to go anymore," Wolflock said flatly, refusing to see how that would impede his friend's goals. "You've said before you wanted to work with people and help them. You've said before you wanted to be a doctor of some sorts. Why are you getting nervous now?"

Mothy bit the side of his lip and played with his vegetables. "I guess I had never really been old enough to analyse a doctor at work." His eyes flashed between Nu and Nan Ji. "I didn't realise how involved the whole process was. Your family studies all day long and still get nervous that they can't help the people around them. I just don't think I'm smart enough to do that and keep up with you."

Nu smiled and laid her hand on his arm. "There are so many things that you think you see but do not, Mothy-mei. I study all day because I love medicine. I love learning about the human body. It is both an amazing... how do you say... puzzle? And it is a beautiful land. All of the little elements coming together to work in perfect harmony. It is my... mìngyùn. It is... It is so hard." Nu huffed and put her palms together, fingertips to her forehead.

"I know the words in Xiayahn. One day you will both learn it and I will be able to show you that I speak much better than you think I do."

Mothy chuckled. "I think you speak beautifully."

"I speak five languages and four of them have a similar root language, so I agree only slightly less than Mothy. You speak well. The more complex and personal aspects of language are complicated and often not taught in classes. You have to be immersed in the culture to get those nuances. Regardless, I believe you mean something along the lines of 'purpose'."

Nu snickered. "Yes. We will move with that. My point is that I study all the time because I love it. There is also not much else I want to read on the ship. I did not go to school. My mother and her parents were my teachers, so my brothers and I were taught by them, which is why we know more than other adults."

Mothy's nervous smile started to become more natural. "My ma taught me too. I learned a bit about herbs."

"Not just herbs. You had to learn all sorts of things and use ingredients I never would have thought of. We use many raw plants and minerals, but you were taught to use ash, grasses and woods in such fascinating ways."

Ash... Wolflock thought, watching Grogen clean out the burnt pieces from the oven. Ash could work like dust.

"I guess I'll see what is available when we reach Mystentine."

Wolflock scanned the room and saw Nan Ji and Stra finishing their meals. He had to hurry.

"Nonsense Mothy." He patted his friend's shoulder absentmindedly. "You're very clever and learned in worldly fashions. Being a doctor will suit you well."

"Thanks, Lockie. Where are you going?"

Without answering him, he slipped into the kitchen area while Grogen began serving the sticky date puddings for dessert. The metal dustpan was still warm from the dead embers. Wolflock shook it to see if anything was still alight, and, upon seeing there wasn't, he moved to the door as if he was taking the waste debris outside.

The lighting was perfect in the dining hall, the floor was smooth and it was a brilliant thoroughfare. It couldn't fail. He pretended to fiddle with the position of the ash tray and brush, waiting for Nan Ji and Stra to rise. He glanced over and saw that they were still finishing their drinks. He'd been too hasty.

"Whoops" he coughed and dropped the tray just enough to spill the ash. The black and grey flecks showered the floor by the door, leaving a perfect dusty puddle across the pathway. The tray hadn't hit the floor though, making his actions only noticed by the people looking. Mothy and Nu raised their eyebrows as they watched his antics.

"I'll just clean this up," he mumbled to no one as he scurried back to the kitchen to pretend to look for a cleaning cloth.

He huffed out his nose as Grogen threw a dishcloth at him. Nan Ji still chortled the last few moments with Stra, drawing out their dinner seating for longer. Wolflock had never dried dishes faster. Every time he finished one he'd glance up to see if Nan Ji had made a move.

He was on his last spoon when Nan Ji finally rose. He and Stra stood up, walked to the door, but Stra seemed to remark on how squeaky the door was. Nan Ji wobbled it back and forth, nodding and scoffing. Wolflock grimaced and rushed over as the men exited the dining hall.

The ash had been blown away by the wind generated by the door. It was then that Wolflock realised, shoulders slumping, that ash for shop prints perhaps wasn't the best idea.

"Did you do this?" Grogen grumbled behind him, making him jump and spin.

"Uhh..."

"Mop is next to the pantry."

Wolflock grinned sheepishly, then shrugged as he grabbed the mop and some clean water, and cleaned up his mess. He'd gotten used to doing the menial tasks asked of him in retribution for his mischief. Making amends as quickly as he could for his misdemeanours allowed him to maintain his continued access to areas other passengers didn't typically try to venture into.

He was also pleased to realise that, whenever he wanted to conduct small experiments, the crew and company were more curious than dismayed. It was freeing to be able to do his little tests without the constant anxiety that he'd be interrupted and embarrass the people around him.

He had a few choices after dinner. He could sneak into Nan Ji's room and check his shoes, but, in the dark with the entire Nan family in there, it would be too risky. He relinquished his plans for the time being and went downstairs to check on Parihaan. She was still unconscious.

He wrote in his journal again, leaving the door open so he could see anyone passing back and forth. It wasn't long before he grew bored. The darkness outside meant he couldn't see any of the passing landscape and there was no music to play.

As he made his mind up to find Haatji and see how her translation was going, Mothy and Nu joined him. Nu tended to her patient and they lingered in the room, talking about this and that. Finally, Mothy started yawning.

"I'm off to bed. I'll see you both in the morning."

"Sleep well." Wolflock waved him off lazily, leaning back in the chair at Parihaan's desk.

"I will take these pins out and go to bed also. I will be awake just before dawn to give her the first dose of medicine for the day." Nu stretched back before settling into taking out the points.

"Mmm..." he hummed, watching everything but not moving as Mothy left.

Nu finished her task and held the thin pins over a flame to sterilise them before wiping them with an alcohol cloth and placing them back in her little, cushioned case.

"Are you standing vigil again tonight?"

Wolflock didn't answer. He just looked to the door. Would the knife person come back again? He kicked his feet off the desk and moved to the window, closing and latching it.

"Why are you so determined to keep watch? I only saw you did not like her or think much of her these past weeks."

Wolflock remained silent for a bit longer. Unable to find anything else to busy himself with, he spoke quietly so no one outside the room could hear.

"I... Nu I don't want to confide this secret with anyone. I'm afraid it will put them in danger. I just know that something is going on that is dangerous. I'm not sure. I... I want to make sure she isn't left alone at any time and there are only a few people I can trust to keep watch."

"Lockie." Nu smiled gently and, for the first time, Wolflock thought she emanated the presence of a true healer. She took up his hands and pressed her thumbs into the webbing of his thumb and index fingers, and her own index finger into the groove on his right in line with his pinkie. Instantly, his shoulders relaxed and his eyes felt weighted. "You need sleep. You will not think as fast or as strong as you normally do if you do not sleep well."

"She needs protecting though."

"You are the master of tricks. Let me show you a dangerous trick women in Xiayah use all the time."

With a curious stare, he watched her disappear into the hallway. He followed her out and stood by Parihaan's door as she came back with a long thin cord of beads and cylindrical bells.

"Put this pin in the corner of the frame and the wall. It should wedge in there strong enough without making an obvious hole."

The lightly tinkling bells made a surprising noise that rang through the silent hallway as Wolflock reached up high and jammed the thicker pin above the door.

"Now," Nu tied the other end of the bells to the door handle, "if anyone tries to open the door, we will hear it loud and clear."

Wolflock put his index knuckle to his chin, thinking. "Let me add one more thing."

He slipped down the stairs to the crew quarters and took a mop. He grabbed his wooden water cups from his bedside table and washing bowl, flipped them upside down, and sat them either side of the door. He then laid the mop across them.

"Now if the bells don't wake us up, the sound of someone tripping over will. Help me take the lanterns away from here so they don't see it."

Nu giggled and put the fairy dust lanterns on his desk. She bid him a good sleep, and although it was a light sleep, it was better than sleeping up against Parihaan's door all night again.

The bells woke Wolflock up. He threw the blanket off himself and bolted out into the cold morning air that had seeped into the hallway. Nu put her fingers to her lips and stepped over the mop trap.

"Pick this up so no one sees this during the day and knows the defences."

Bleary eyed and dehydrated, Wolflock nodded and collected the cups and mop before laying back down on his bed and falling back asleep with his arm over the mop.

It felt like seconds later that something touched his ear. He swatted it away. It touched it again. He grumbled and left his arm over it. The thing tickled his palm.

"Be gone," he groaned and rolled over.

"Oh, don't be like that," Mothy snickered. "You'll miss out on breakfast."

Grouchy, Wolflock glared back at his friend and rolled out of bed. "I'm not even hungry."

"You're never hungry. Someone has to remind you to eat, though, and I will nobly take on the role of caretaker for the Prince of the Silver Ice Hair."

"You realise when we get to Mystentine I'm going to make you nobility of the most ridiculous things as payback, right?"

"I only look forward to it, my liege. Now, come along. I'm starving."

Wolflock got dressed in his warmer attire and they made their way to the dining hall, saying good morning to Veluse as they passed him painting the midmorning landscape. The buckets at his feet and the way he used his handprints for clouds gave Wolflock an idea.

"What are our brilliant plans for the day?" Mothy chimed in as they collected their bread, eggs and leftover vegetables for breakfast.

"I was thinking I'd see if Veluse could teach me to paint. I'm not skilled with colours and I thought it would be handy to understand the viscosity and manufacturing of paints for our studies."

Mothy looked thoughtful for a moment. "That sounds like a fine idea. I used to do finger painting in the mud, so this will be a charming step up."

Wolflock laughed, happy to have Mothy's company. He hadn't realised just how lonely he'd felt these past few days. After breakfast, the boys made their way back out onto the deck and took a stroll to digest their food. They then approached Veluse. It made Wolflock pleased to see that Nan Ji had taken up his normal position smoking with Stra on the mid deck.

"Merry meet, Veluse," he said, admiring the way the artist had captured the shades of light through the pass.

"Why young Mr Felen! And Mothy! How are you this day? Not too sombre I hope?" He beamed with a quick flick of his wrist, creating sparse pine tree silhouettes.

"Are we well?" Wolflock looked at Mothy.

"I believe we are," Mothy nodded back.

"We were wondering if you would teach us about painting. Could we help you and get a few instructions? I'm very fascinated in the process for research purposes."

"And I think it looks beautiful."

"Would you show us how you do your work if we helped you?"

Veluse looked confused for a moment before laughing from his belly. "Why, of course, my boys! I've just about finished this one, but we can paint a few others. Carry this bucket and we'll find the perfect spot!"

"Can I choose it?" Wolflock asked quickly.

Veluse winked and rolled up his leather pouch of brushes. "Only this one time."

Wolflock requested the most likely place that Nan Ji was going to walk through back to the cabins and dining hall at the middle of the ship.

"Hmmm... Yes. Yes, I like it. I've been so caught up with the transient scenes around the ship, that I completely forgot the ship itself from this angle is rather majestic. I'm sure it's something no other artist has played with on their canvas before. Like the paintings of a flower's stigma and style, rather than the petals and leaves. Yes, yes, yes!"

Mothy held up his thumbs and index fingers, framing different locations on the ship with one eye shut, whereas Wolflock put his knuckle to his chin, considering the density of the paint and its ability to take imprints.

"Now, boys, get some water with the bucket and we'll mix up some happy paints to show the magic of this scene."

Wolflock filled the bucket with chilly river water and brought it back. The other passengers were passing around the deck frequently while others played card games. Tinni was trying to get Gege and Didi to play a clapping game, but they couldn't get the timing right.

"Good, good! Now, white is what we have in abundance and is one of the most useful colours, so I want you to mix five parts water to one part of this white. We'll be using this one a lot. Then get another bucket and we'll mix one part blue to ten parts water. That will be the base so we can blend! It gives the illusion of silveriness."

Wolflock and Mothy spent a good three hours going back and forth for Veluse, getting him water for his powdered paints and listening to him prattle on about brush strokes, blending and symbolism. All the while Wolflock kept analysing the paint consistencies and the waste water bucket, testing out the markings on the small canvas Veluse had given him.

"Now blue is a tricky colour to find, but not too rare when you know how to make it. Red is so very common. You can get it everywhere. It's the metallic colours that are actual pieces of art to find. Silver, gold and copper are so hard to make into good quality paints that you may as well just melt the metals onto the canvas yourself! And then of course purple..."

"How would you make metallic paints, though?" Wolflock probed, looking up from his messy canvas.

Veluse put, his index finger to his lips as he thought, leaving orange and blue paint on it absentmindedly.

"Well... I haven't used it much, but it normally is made with insect shells or metal particles. The only one I've seen before was from nail paint, you know? For fingernails. It takes so long to dry though, so it has to be a very well-to-do person who just talks and never uses their hands. That's the only way to accomplish those perfect results. I remember this one gentleman who was obsessed with gold, Sadim, from Uluken. He lived in Corl and spent all day having his nails painted golden so he could say he had a 'touch of gold'. Boring self absorbed chap who even painted his lap dog's nails gold too…"

This went on and on for what felt like an age.

"One of the most important lessons of all is to have someone to paint for. If you have a higher purpose, you will never have a lack of inspiration. Who are you both painting for?"

Mothy made a face as he added an outline to his fish. "I'm painting this for Tinni. She said she wanted a pet fish, so this can do while she travels."

"I hadn't thought about that. I might paint this for…" Wolflock thought hard. "Parihaan."

Veluse scoffed. "Paint it for someone worthwhile, Mr Felen. She wouldn't appreciate it unless it was gilded in gold and lined with prayers."

"Pardon?"

"I'm just saying that some muses will dry up. Find a person worthy of your growing skills. I can see you're going for a… a maramuti?"

"I was thinking about a horse," Wolflock said flatly. "What is your disapproval of Miss Nebralt?"

"She and I had serious disagreements on fundamental human roles and what one may call divine."

"Oh?"

"It's nothing. Nothing to get stuck into, anyway. Just a few verbal tête-à-têtes. That's all. Those lessons can be a fantastic source of growth and inspiration though! As my master used to say..."

He bestowed the artistic wisdom of the ages on them, boring Wolflock to no end with anecdotal prattle. He couldn't ignore that Veluse had also had strong feelings about Parihaan's behaviour, though. It itched at the back of his brain just how passionately Veluse had dismissed her as a worthy reciprocant of Wolflock's pretend artwork. What disagreements had they had? Was he a thread in this web of evidence Wolflock had missed? Just as he was listening to Veluse talking about mistakes turning into birds, Nan Ji rose with Stra.

"I'll get you some clean water for your brush!" Wolflock jumped to his feet, grabbing the bucket of dirty water, thick with paint sediment at the bottom.

"But you just cleaned it-"

It was too late. Wolflock kicked the bucket of blue paint across the pale deck, right into Nan Ji's path. He and Stra stepped into it, hissing.

"Clumsy boy!"

"Sorry!" He feigned a gasp and crawled over to them to collect the scattered brushes. "Sorry!"

Nan Ji took a step back and Wolflock saw a pristine impression from his and Stra's shoes. "Quick, Wolflock, quick! Get me a big bucket of water. We'll have to soak this up before it stains the wood!" Veluse cried out as he and Mothy, whose shirt was now covered in orange paint, rushed around to clean the blue mess.

"Come with me, Ji," Stra smiled and put his hand on Nan Ji's shoulder. "I have a tonic that clears guts and paints like soap cleans mud."

They both left quickly with Nan Ji grumbling in his native language.

Wolflock smiled from ear to ear, whipping out his notebook and scribbling down the shoe design.

Veluse rushed over with a bucket of water, but he held up his hand to stop him. "Wait!"

"What, Wolflock? What?"

"I'm inspired! I must capture this!"

Veluse and Mothy both froze. Mothy grinning, Veluse looking perplexed but also excited.

"There! Very well. Wash it away."

And with that the blue was rinsed from the ship. Wolflock looked over his drawing in great detail while Veluse recovered from the mess and loss of his blue paint.

Nan Ji's shoes had a squared geometrical pattern with no hint of floral work at all. Stra's shoes had a typical slanted cut to them and a diamond shape underneath the ball. The pattern didn't match. To make matters worse, the graphite in his pencil had shattered and was coming out in pieces.

"I'm sorry, Veluse. Maybe painting just isn't for me," Wolflock shrugged with a frown, waving at his abstract canvas.

Veluse seemed unperturbed by this and put his hand on Wolflock's shoulder as he tilted his head back and forth at the soiled canvas. "It is an odd design, but not unworthy of being called art. You may want to stick to sketching shoes though. You seem to have a talent for it."

"You wouldn't have another pencil on you?" Wolflock asked, showing the artist the shards of his broken one.

"Pop downstairs. I think I left a jar of them on my bedside table."

With a nod, Wolflock trotted downstairs into Veluse's open room. There were no pencils on his bedside table or desk, so he opened the desk draw. Jars of metallic paint rolled right to his hand.

Veluse had lied. He said he didn't have any metallic paints. But there were gold, copper, and silver before him. Silver...

Wolflock snatched a pencil out of the drawer and

rushed to his room. He added his new pictures to his notes, sketching down Nan Ji's shoe print several times over to make sure he'd gotten it right. His mind buzzed. Nan Ji may not be the culprit, but now he had a shining silver thread of potential motives and evidence.

Had the artist attempted murder?

Rhiannon D. Elton

CHAPTER 9

Clean Crimes

Wolflock found that pacing around the deck before lunch was the most helpful way to organise his thoughts. No one bothered him since Mothy had continued painting for the rest of the morning.

On the night Parihaan had been pushed down the stairs, Veluse appeared to be in his room. When Wolflock had come up from the hull he had poked his head out of his cabin. Wolflock remembered his silk nightcap. He couldn't prove Veluse had been in his room when Parihaan had been pushed down the stairs. Wolflock had also noticed his expression during that time was odd. He seemed to be blinking too much. Was he conscious of it? Was it his way of trying not to look suspicious? It was certainly odd. Had Parihaan been prejudiced against his lifestyle? His career? His choice of partner?

The thought that she could be a bigot and that Wolflock was trying to bring her justice squirmed in his gut. He pushed it away by thinking that, regardless of her previous actions, she still required justice. As would any being.

Veluse always wore long sleeves, so it would be difficult to see if he had scratches on his arm. He did have the metallic paint though. Did he have a trace of it on his hands the night Parihaan fell?

Then there was the strange behaviour of Captain Blutro. Parihaan had smuggled alcohol onboard, caused one of his crew to lie to him, and reminded him of his brother's torment and death. That was a clear motive enough. The ship was also decorated with all types of silver, some of which was definitely painted. In order to keep the ship looking as trim and fresh as it did, someone would have to repaint some of it. He'd have to find if there was any paint for detailing aboard, but he wasn't allowed in the hull anymore. That would be the only place he'd imagine it would be kept.

If he could get a sample of the paint used on the ship

he could compare it to Veluse's paint and see which matched the silver on Parihaan.

But Nu had washed Parihaan. There wouldn't be anymore paint on her. He stood up straight as he realised where there was still a sample of the paint. The wall and railing in the hull. He'd have to sneak down with a handkerchief and a scraping tool to collect it.

He went down to his room and found a pen knife in his stationary. It would certainly do. He put it in his pocket just as he heard Haatji finish her midday prayers. He pulled out the pages of shoe prints and glanced over them alongside Parihaan's diary pages. The threads were coming together. Veluse or the Captain would definitely have a pair of shoes as flamboyant as the floral soled ones. They had associations with silver and possible motives, enough to push Parihaan down the stairs. He just needed a bit more data and he would have this case cracked.

"Mr Felen?" Haatji tapped his door frame, peering into his room.

"Haatji! Perfect. How has the translation proceeded?"

She scratched the tip of her nose through the fabric of her glittering orange niqab. "It... it was very reminiscent of home. I am finished, but the first entry will require a little more work as there are quite a few terms that are specific to Uluken. I am very pleased I could help you with this. Understanding the people we often vilify makes them far more... human."

"Do you mean because she was a drunk or because she was a Troston?"

"Both, actually. May I give you some context?"

"Absolutely. Here. Have a seat."

He turned his chair out and sat on the edge of his bed. He'd seen his father do this with foreign dignitaries to help them warm up to him, as well as seen Mothy do it to comfort others. For some reason, sacrificing your seat was a universal sign of respect in a self aggrandizing fashion.

Haatji lowered herself into the seat with a straight spine and smoothed out her intricate dress.

"In Uluken, we celebrate the fifteen primordial gods, local elements and the Great Mother. The temples we built for each of them are elaborate and protected with extravagant care. Uluken is very dry and very hot, though, so the god we seek the favour and kindness of is the god of the sands, Enlil'Nunamnir. One of the masculine gods, he rules the desert and calls for storms. He is the brightness of the sun that makes the sands hard to gaze upon. He breathes the wind and reshapes the earth in Uluken as he sees fit. Normally, we offer him a portion of our meals in special altars by the windows.

"The bigger temples will offer fruits and meats to his vulture messengers. Spiritually, when we are in abundance, it is nice to feed the creatures of the desert. Scientifically, they take the seeds and meat and fertilize the oases with their droppings and propagate the plants through the desert."

Wolflock blinked. She understood the practicality of the spiritual purposes in her country. Not many people bothered to learn them, and it took him by surprise that this woman he'd expected to just be a socialite would know them.

"We also have a distinct branch of the Troston faith amongst us. They refuse to participate in any of the cultural activities because it is against their laws, which is fine. Each to their own," the more she spoke the more Wolflock picked up on her lisp. "There are small places of worship for them, which is all the law requires."

"How does this relate to Parihaan?"

"People do not like them in Uluken. Even those that leave their faith have a hard time settling into normal society. Part of the reason they don't like them is the amount of water they use for their sacrificial alcohol."

"I don't know much about the practices, to be honest. Sacrificial alcohol?"

"They will spill goblets of red alcohol to symbolise

the spilling of their leader's blood. I don't fully understand it myself, but it takes gallons of water to raise the grapes in the desert, so to pour it out feels like such a terrible waste. Even worse, the alcohol makes it harder for the other places and animals to grow near it. It's their self deprecating waste of precious resources that makes them disliked. Due to this, they set up communes and villages of their own so they can practice in peace."

"I have heard they like to do that." Wolflock shuffled uncomfortably, thinking about Mothy.

"Parihaan was raised in one of these communes. The way they treated her and... I just have a new understanding of her. We are more similar than I originally thought. I do ask, though, when you read it, please take this as a very unique example. There are more people in Uluken that are kind, intelligent and offer levels of hospitality that would warm the hearts of all those who pass through. I..." She paused, looking to the door, "I am proud of my people and I just didn't want you to think that this behaviour was normal. Even I am an anomaly in Uluken. You will have to visit one day and you will see."

"What do you mean you're an anomaly?"

"My situation back home is unique as well. I think that was why I was so mad when Parihaan was talking about a woman's place in the world. I am the eldest daughter of the Semiramis family. We are one of the oldest, most noble families in Uluken. I have been trained all my life to uphold the strengths of women and be an example of their intelligence, compassion, power and resourcefulness. I was so angered when Parihaan slandered her sex that I didn't stop to think she may not have ever known any better."

"I see," Wolflock nodded, feeling his chest tighten uncomfortably. He was one of the noble households of Plugh and he never thought he had any duties whatsoever. Was Myna raised differently to him? She certainly understood the expectation of the family name far more than he did.

"Regardless, here are your pages. I should finish the last one tomorrow morning. What are you working on?"

Haatji turned in the chair and placed the transcribed letters on the scattered pile of notes. Wolflock stood up and felt relieved she had been so forthcoming and helpful. He missed having someone to confide in since he didn't want to endanger Mothy. Surely, Haatji wasn't in the same danger his friend was.

He couldn't, though. What if he would put her in danger by telling her?

"It's just some notes I took to get the image out of my head. There were a lot of little details and I found that by focusing on them I can't see... Well... I don't think of how she looked."

Haatji stared at the notes, her eyes passing slowly around his desk. "I hope these entries help to clear your mind, as they did mine." She stood up and floated to the door, turning sideways to look at his one last time. "I hope they help you understand that no one is unworthy of forgiveness."

Wolflock nodded as she left, then filed his sketches and the new diary entries into his journal. It was starting to get too thick for his pocket, so he put it into his bedside table drawer and took a few new pages and a pen for his note taking. He checked on Parihaan, only to find Geagle writing at her desk.

"Is she well?"

"Oh! Mr Wolflock, sir! Yes sir."

"Excellent. Would you assist me for a moment, Geagle?"

"Yes sir, of course, sir. Is it to help my darling Pari-rose?"

Wolflock felt nauseous from Geagle's pet names. "Yes. I'm not meant to go into the hull alone, so would you accompany me for just a few minutes?"

Geagle thought for a moment, slowly weighing up whether the information was credible, or possibly contemplating what his next rhyme would be. Wolflock couldn't tell.

"Just a few minutes. I'm sure the Captain wouldn't mind."

"Of course not," Wolflock lied.

He followed Geagle down into the hull. When he saw the landing in the hull he pushed passed Geagle and stared in horror.

Spotless.

The dust along the sides of the floor were wiped clean. So were the railings. This place hadn't been cleaned the entire time he had been on the ship. Why had it been cleaned now? And when? By who?

"What happened?" he gasped.

"What's going on down there, Geagle?" Goden grumbled from the top of the stairs, "Ain't you meant to be doing games 'bout now? What in the-"

He spotted Wolflock and huffed, putting down the barrel he was hauling.

"Mr Felen. Git outta there righ' now!"

"Goden? When did someone clean the landing to the hull? It's not normal," Wolflock asked as he ascended the stairs again.

"Hmm? Yeh... Cap'in asked me to take care o' it. Clear the bad 'nergy out 'n all. Now off wit' cha, lad. I told yeh ta stay outta here. I won't ask again. Don't you be letting him trick yeh neither, Geagle."

"Yes sir. Sorry sir."

Wolflock trudged back to his room and scribbled more in his journal. A cleansing of the area a person had had a terrible accident was normal, especially in a place as superstitious as a ship, but it nagged at him that things were not as easy as they had been. He supposed it was doubly hard because of the Captain's prejudice against him pursuing the case. As well as not being able to confide in Mothy.

He was reaching a point where he needed more help though. He put away his journal and decided it was time. He had two people he needed to check for clues and he needed more help. They weren't just going to ask him to walk into their cabins and find evidence against them.

"What are you up to, Lockie?"

Wolflock jumped, turning to see Mothy leaning against the doorframe.

"Pardon?"

"What are you up to?" Mothy repeated, his smile becoming a smirk. "You're not interested in painting. You certainly aren't that clumsy. You have been chatting secretly with Nü and you've been drawing shoe prints for days. Are you going to tell me what you're up to or do I have to guess?"

Wolflock sighed. Maybe it was a sign.

"You're right. Let me show you." He reached for his bedside drawer.

"Mr Felen, I'd like to see you in my study," Captain Blutro suddenly appeared next to Mothy looking stern.

"Uh... yes Captain." Wolflock nodded as the captain walked away again. Looking at Mothy he shrugged. "I'll have to show you later."

"I'll meet you for tea in the kitchen. Good luck. He looks cranky," Mothy chuckled and gave him a supportive pat on the shoulder.

He was ten paces behind Captain Blutro until they reached his stateroom. The captain didn't offer him a seat, nor did he sit at the little table in the middle of the room over the secret grate Wolflock and Mothy had used for all manner of mischief. The broad shouldered man sat behind his large desk, making Wolflock stand at attention in front of him.

"Do you explicitly ignore my instructions to irritate me or terrify me, Mr Felen?"

Wolflock held his tongue to think of a response. "I'd say neither, Captain."

"Then why do you do it?"

"Higher calling?" he shrugged.

Aujin the snuffle unwrapped himself from the

Captain's bald head and face, and slithered along the table to get chin scratches from Wolflock. Captain Blutro sighed.

"I understand that you've been pursuing a line of questioning and activities that have made other people aboard the ship feel uncomfortable."

"Geagle? You do realise we're good friends now. Very chummy."

"And others."

"What others?"

"That doesn't matter. This needs to stop, Mr. Felen. You've been trespassing, interrogating and possibly even stealing. Thievery will not be tolerated aboard my vessel. Do I make myself clear?"

"But attempted murder is?"

"You need to understand that the ship is going through an unprecedented hard time and we don't need these wounds opened anymore. What's done is done, regardless of how it happened. All we can do now is heal from it."

"I find that wounds don't heal unless they're cleaned, Captain," Wolflock scoffed.

Captain Blutro glared at him with the authority of a glacier over a dingy. "I like you, Mr Felen. I've given you privileges aboard my vessel that I'd not extend to most. Do not make me regret my faith in you."

Those last few words stung. Wolflock broke their staring match, looking about the room. He could check to see if the Captain had scratches on his arm. He could also do it while pretending to call a truce.

He hesitated, though. He didn't want to believe that the Captain had performed such a heinous crime. Wolflock liked the Captain. He was one of the first people to request his investigative services and had believed that he could accomplish them, even if he was reluctant about the means. Wolflock couldn't let it go though. He couldn't deliver his message that may have saved Parihaan that night. The least he could do was find her justice.

"Very well. I'll stop searching, Captain. I did complete the previous task you charged me with, though. Parihaan was the smuggler, but I do not think for a moment she was the mastermind. I found a note suggesting she was just encouraged by someone else. I'm not sure if they are on the ship or not, but those are my findings."

"I appreciate your work. My apologies for not trusting you as you went about your investigation. I didn't know who to trust and when I felt as if the only person I could confide in was hiding things from me... well... I'm sorry it brought out a colder side of me."

"Does that mean I don't have to do the labour you

were punishing me with?"

Captain Blutro chuckled as Aujin nestled under his hand on the desk. "I will remove it from your record."

"Thank you. If it's not too much to ask, can I request a small reward for my services? That makes this my first successful job. Just something to write home to my sister about."

Captain Blutro frowned in thought, then nodded. "It depends on the request. What did you have in mind?"

"Can I try on your coat?"

Captain Blutro rolled his eyes with a smile and took off his dark blue, silver trimmed knee length jacket. He passed it to Wolflock and he put his arms into it, flicking up the ostentatious high collar.

"Here. You'll see yourself better here," Captain Blutro opened his closet door to reveal a full length mirror.

The coat was a bit too large, but it was the kind of garment that would look good on anyone.

"There's nothing in the pockets, by the way, so don't bother searching it."

"I would never!" Wolflock gasped incredulously.

The captain chuckled and leaned on the cupboard. As he folded his arms Wolflock watched him scratch at them.

"Do you have a matching hat?"

Without a word, the captain took a matching three pointed hat off the top of the cupboard and plopped it onto Wolflock's head. He looked quite dashing.

"Are your arms injured?" he asked, seeing the Captain scratch at his arms from his peripheries.

"Hmm? No. Well... Nothing serious."

When Wolflock was finished preening, he turned to the captain and returned the coat and hat.

"Is it a rash?"

"No, Wolflock."

"Will you show me? Just to soothe my nerves. I have a terrible phobia of getting a rash."

"I don't believe that for a moment. I would have thought your only phobia would be to lose your tongue."

"Perhaps it's just my way of showing concern."

Captain Blutro rolled his eyes and tugged his sleeves up. His arms were covered in scratches.

"I'll be honest with you, Mr Felen. I scratch my arms incessantly in my sleep when I'm under great stress. This drinking alcohol business has brought up a lot of sour old memories and I'm glad it's over and done with."

The scratches on both arms did indeed look older than a few days, but Wolflock was still suspicious.

"How do you keep the silver on the ship so stunning? Do you have something to touch it up if it gets damaged?" Wolflock looked around the room, admiring the cornice.

"We have a bit of wall paint, but don't go touching it. It's expensive and hard to source. It can take a whole passenger's travel fare to pay for a half gallon. That's why the crew are careful not to damage the ship. They take pride in their work and I expect you to as well."

Wolflock nodded thoughtfully. "Indeed. Thank you for the use of your coat."

They parted and Wolflock closed the Captain's stateroom door, wondering if he had the coldness required to push someone down the stairs. Did he hate Parihaan that much? None of the crew would ever reveal his secret. If he took on the Captain he'd be taking on the whole ship and his own fondness for the man.

As he made his way down the hallway he barely noticed the person at his door calling to him.

"Mr Felen!"

Haatji came close to him, only able to break through his thoughts by touching his shoulder. He looked up and brought his mind back to the present moment.

"Mr Felen! Your room!"

"My room?"

"I... oh dear... I do not know who did it..."

He pushed passed her and slid to a halt outside his

door.

It was ransacked. And his papers were gone.

"I was just here though. I was away with the Captain for just a few minutes!"

"I'm so sorry. Is everything there?" Haatji asked nervously with her hands to her lips.

Wolflock began throwing things around.

"My journal! All my notes! Where are they!?"

He had only been gone a few minutes. Who would have had time to do this? They'd have to be standing outside his door from the time he left, surely...

But that meant the only person who could have done this was...

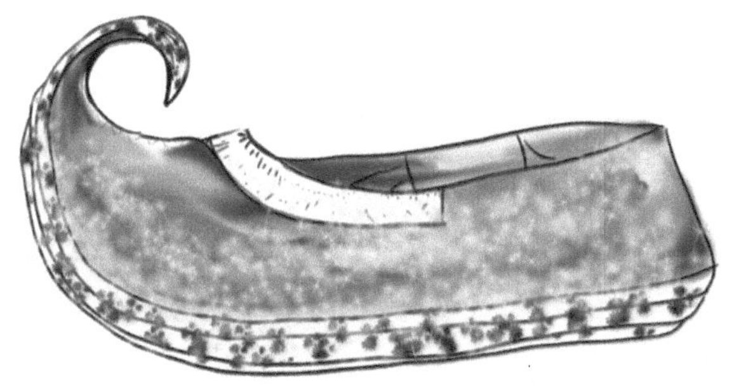

CHAPTER 10

An Innocent Thief

"Mothy..." Wolflock breathed.

It didn't add up though. Why would his best friend do this to his room? Where was he?

A cold voice in the back of his mind dropped a piece of the puzzle into place that he hadn't wanted to see before. Mothy didn't have an alibi for the time Parihaan was pushed down the stairs. He had dark secrets in his past that would have prepared him for something as terrible as attempted murder.

His palms were small even though his fingers were long. His feet weren't particularly large for a boy his size either. If the drinking alcohol had come from slavers or even a slave related industry, then Mothy may have been tipped over the edge and snapped.

The image of Mothy's eyes going dark brown and his fist clenched in rage when Parihaan had her altercation with the other passengers on the top deck flashed through his mind. Had he been deliberately ignoring that his best friend could have been a suspect? Was that the reason he hadn't confided in him?

It couldn't be, though. Not Mothy. Not the eternally optimistic, irritatingly happy Mothy... Not his friend.

Wolflock caught the edge of his desk as his head swam with terrible accusations.

Mothy knew of the secret tunnels and passageways throughout the ship, too. What if there was one he knew about from the hull to the deck or to the cabins. He would have been in and out of there without anyone ever noticing. Was it that premeditated, though? Was it just a quickly thought out opportunity when he saw her head to the hull?

"Are you well, Mr Felen?" Haatji asked, holding up her hand as if she wanted to comfort him, but drew it back as he nodded.

"I'm fine. I'm just bothered that I have to clean my room, is all. You didn't happen to see how this happened did you?"

"No. I did not. I was in my room and then came to see how you fared with the entries I had given to you earlier to find this." She waved her hand about the room. "Have you upset someone?"

Wolflock picked up one of his shirts and tossed it onto the desk. He couldn't lie that it was a bit suspicious that Haatji had been in his room just as he'd found it in disarray.

"May I see your arm, Miss Semiramis?"

"Pardon?"

"It's purely to prove your innocence in the matter."

"My innocence? What matter?"

Wolflock sighed and laid his mattress back onto the bed, straightening his bedding as he spoke. "In the matter of who searched my room. You see, the person who searched my belongings knows that I'm onto them and they're frightened. If you show me your forearm I will have no reason to suspect you."

Haatji frowned, but very carefully peeled back her sleeve to show her right arm up to her elbow, trying to not get her freshly painted nails bumped on the fabric. "Satisfied?"

There were no scratches.

"Thank you. It is good to know for certain I have

someone I can trust in."

"I'm glad you feel that way. What is plaguing you, though?"

"It's nothing, Haatji. I... I just... Nothing..."

"Please come up to afternoon tea. You don't look well. It will do you good," she soothed.

"I'll be up soon. I just need to clean this up first."

She nodded and withdrew, leaving him to get his room in order.

As he picked up the discarded notes from his missing journal, he let his mind fixate on the mental web before him. Haatji was clear. She had an alibi from Faleen and Bleen, she also didn't have any scratches on her arm from where Parihaan would have injured her.

The Captain did have scratches. Veluse and Mothy, he hadn't yet seen.

The three of them didn't have an alibi for the time when Parihaan was pushed down the stairs. They each had been upset by her to an intense degree. Although the Captain hadn't ransacked his room directly, he might have drawn Wolflock away to send one of the crew to do it. Veluse and Mothy had access to it the entire time he was with Captain Blutro.

Wolflock hung his clothes back up and put away his belongings piece by piece. His mind whirled with every moment he had ever spent with Mothy, wondering if there had been some small sign he had wilfully missed.

There was.

When he asked Nu where Parihaan's silver flask was Mothy had scratched his nose. He didn't even need to speak and he was lying. If he found the flask in Mothy's room or on his person it would mean... what would it mean? That Mothy found it laying around somewhere? That he'd been too embarrassed to return it?

That he'd taken it from her after he'd pushed her down the stairs?

He had to find it. He couldn't let it rest. Besides, if Mothy had ransacked his room, it was only fair that Wolflock got to snoop around his.

He slipped into Mothy's bare cabin and thought to himself.

If I were Mothy and I'd taken something from someone I wasn't fond of, where would I hide it? In my bag? No. That would be too obvious. Plus, if there was a suspected thief on board it would be the first place someone would look. The bedside table and desk aren't of interest to me except for the use of the available stationary, but not mine personally. I would hide it... in the mattress.

Wolflock lifted the bedding up and smiled. No flask. Were his instincts off? He surely hoped so.

Then something fell out of the tucked sheet with a thud on the wooden panels beneath. Something silver and heavy. Parihaan's full flask.

"Mothy..." Wolflock groaned, putting the bed down again. So, it was true. He grimaced, turning his head to the left.

Something sparkling caught his eye. The reflection of something golden and shimmering bounced off the open porthole window. Everything on the Silver Ice Hair was silver, not gold. Why would something outside the ship be gold?

Wolflock went to the window and looked down. A pair of black, curled toed shoes with gold beads glinting in the afternoon sunlight. They were hanging by a cord that had caught on a warped plank of the ship, keeping them pinned together. He reached out and grabbed them, fumbling for a moment as he'd gone numb from his realisations.

He flipped the shoe over and saw the intricate floral print he'd been looking for. Mothy had two damning pieces of evidence pinning the attempted murder on him. Had he been the one with the knife? Wolflock couldn't bear to comprehend it. He felt sick. He had to confront him. Maybe he would turn himself in to the Captain and just get a term of indenturement. Maybe he'd be taken to the nearest guard tower... Wolflock's throat tightened. His best friend had grown up as a prisoner, he couldn't be the reason Mothy became one again. He had to speak to him.

The shadows cast across the river told him it wasn't dinner time yet, but, if Mothy wasn't on deck, he'd be helping make the food so he could scrounge extra.

With the shoes in hand, Wolflock made his way to the dining hall. Mothy was eating dates behind Geagle's back as the crewman tried to make a type of sweet curry. He bit his lip with a furrowed brow. Perhaps if he turned around now, he could pretend that he came in by accident. He didn't have enough evidence. There was no point interrogating him about it until he had more data. He was just about to turn and leave when Mothy spotted him.

"Lockie! Come help us make dinner."

Wincing, Wolflock shuffled over. Mothy handed him a freshly acquired date.

"What's the matter? You look like the Captain gave you a thorough telling off and took away your deck privileges again."

"Umm... Where were you the night Parihaan fought with everyone on the deck?"

"Huh? I was up here with Nü and her brothers watching the stars. I wanted you to join us, but I couldn't find you after you left the dining hall."

"Was that really where you were? Nu said you came and joined them later. How long after Parihaan fought with everyone did you join them?"

Mothy looked up, thinking. "Not too long. Maybe an hour. Maybe less."

Wolflock's heart sank. Did Mothy not realise he was digging for suspicious information? He'd just removed his alibi.

"You look off. Here, I got you some afternoon tea. There wasn't much to choose from but I thought you'd prefer the salad sandwich over the tuna surprise. I think the surprise was Tuiti fruit jam. Geagle? Where are the clean plates?"

"In the barrel, soaking."

"No worries." Mothy tipped his fingers from his forehead to Geagle and pushed his sleeves up to retrieve a plate from the water. Wolflock saw his arms.

"Mothy... How did you get those scratches?"

"Huh? Oh these? I got them from Parihaan."

A cold pit dropped in his stomach. How could Mothy be so nonchalant about it? He was admitting to being the cause of her injuries.

"What do you mean?"

"Remember when she left that night?" His voice dropped so Geagle couldn't hear him, "I wanted to go and speak to her about how she spoke to Nu and try to get her to apologise or at least get treatment. I caught her just outside her cabin and she grabbed my arm, falling over. Her nails were really jagged and tore me up. She didn't listen to me though, so I dropped it."

That was a terrible cover story.

"Have you seen these before?" Wolflock put the shoes on the kitchen counter.

"Did you pick these up from the Krieger Zwerg markets?" Mothy picked one up curiously.

"Oi! Get that off!" Geagle gasped, flinging his arms across the counter and knocking the shoe to the ground. "Old shoes on a table bring death!"

"I don't think it's that old," Wolflock sniffed.

"New shoes bring babies! Either way, we don' want 'em on the ship!"

Wolflock raised his hands in surrender, letting Geagle know he could go back to his cooking without any fear of death or babies suddenly appearing on the ship. There was no point arguing with crewmates about superstitions.

"It's a pretty shoe, and I appreciate the gesture, but I don't think they'll fit me. They're a little bit small."

"Can you humour me and try to wedge your foot in anyway?"

Mothy smirked and slipped the pristine shoe onto his grubby foot. It only just fit.

"It's too uncomfortable, Lockie. You'll have to get me a bigger size next time. It's a very pretty shoe, though. What's this about?"

"It was hanging outside your window." He had to tell him. It ached within his chest to keep it hidden any longer. "It matches the footprints I found on the landing when I discovered Parihaan."

Mothy's green eyes looked from the shoe, back to Wolflock, then back to the shoe.

"Parihaan also had blood under her nails."

Mothy nodded slowly, still not comprehending what Wolflock was saying.

"I also found this after my room was pillaged."

He pulled out the silver flask from his jacket pocket. Mothy's face finally flushed pink at seeing it.

"That one I can explain."

Wolflock leaned back on the bench and crossed his arms expectantly. "Go on then."

"I saw the flask when I went to confront Parihaan in front of her cabin. She hurled a torrent of abuse at me, then took a swig of this. I knew there was drinking alcohol in it, so I slipped it out of her hand as she went into her room. She was so out of it that she didn't even notice. I just didn't want her to keep drinking from it. You know?"

Wolflock wanted it to make sense, but the shoes were a damning piece of evidence.

"Why didn't you hand it in? Or tell me you had it?"

Mothy shrugged with a guilty grin, "I forgot I had it after breakfast the morning after. I also didn't want Nu to know I'd gotten hurt from Parihaan. She has enough to worry about."

"If that is so, then why were these tossed out of your window? And why was my room plundered right after I left you?"

"Lockie," Mothy said patronisingly, "I have one pair of shoes to my name. They're a decent quality, but I only have one. Shoes are heavy to lug around. I don't know why they were tossed out my window, but someone must have been on to you being onto them if they were trying to get rid of these. The same person probably went through your room. I headed right up here to wait for you to tell me what you've been up to over the last few days because I was worried about you."

Wolflock scratched at his upper arm, unable to look Mothy in the eye. "And now I'm worried about you."

"The shoe thing?"

"Aye, the shoe thing."

The blond boy frowned in thought for a few

moments, rubbing his chin and looking around as he twisted his foot back and forth of the new shoe. "Ahah!" he exclaimed and took the flour sack from the pantry. "I saw you do this with ash the other day and it had me intrigued. Let me tell you now that flour works way better. You need a good fine flour though."

Mothy started dusting the kitchen tiles with the flour, glancing up at Geagle every now and then to make sure he wasn't about to stop them.

"Very well, my prince. Would you kindly give us the first demonstration of flour foot analysis?"

Wolflock couldn't help but chuckle, and he walked casually across the thin layer of flour. Mothy was right, it was quite a good way to track prints. His own shoes were cleanly outlined and when he stepped out of the flour the white powder tracked him for a few more steps. What was more, Wolflock could determine the size of his stride and stance.

"This got me in a lot of trouble in the kitchens down South. I tried to use it to prove it wasn't one of us stealing stewed fruits. Even with proof they didn't believe us though."

Wolflock nodded slowly, watching Mothy as he put the second tight shoe on and walked back and forth away from the flour to get a natural step. Mothy's gait was longer than Wolflock's, but his toes were more forward. Not a single one of Mothy's footprints came out clearly. Every step he took smudged as he twisted his toes outwards.

"How curious!"

"It was the only way to stop the masters from finding out who had stolen food or supplies. They couldn't trace our footprints so they couldn't tell if it was one of us or if it was one of their own. It didn't normally stop the punishments, but it did keep a few of us safe and fed."

"Indeed. Now, stand with your legs to the bench. Heels against it."

Moth shrugged and did as he was told. Wolflock positioned himself in front of his friend and braced himself.

"Now try to push me over."

"What?"

"Push me over. Go on. Do this and I'll have the data I need."

Mothy grinned awkwardly and reached out to shove Wolflock's shoulders. The kitchen tiles were slipperier than Wolflock had calculated due to the flour. His feet slipped out from under him and he fell in a heap. Mothy came toppling down on him laughing.

Wolflock shoved him off and scrambled to his feet. "Don't move!"

Mothy's feet had done their strange twist even while he was preoccupied. He really wasn't aware of the twist when he did it. It was his default state of walking. The person who had originally worn the floral patterned black shoes had stood poised. They had been still enough to leave a perfect imprint that was clear enough for Wolflock to memorize and sketch.

His shoulders relaxed.

"Thank goodness."

"Are you going to tell me what this is all about now? Or do I have to roll you through the flour again? You look like a baker!"

Wolflock chuckled and dusted himself down.

"No, no. I'm happy to tell you. Just... not here. Come on outside."

"Give me a hand up then!"

Wolflock grinned and reached out to Mothy, who gripped him around the forearm to be hoisted up. Grateful to have his friend to confide in, Wolflock told Mothy everything. They made their way around the deck for ten laps before Wolflock finished his explanation. How he was suspicious of Haatji to begin with, but that the twins, Faleen and Bleen, had given her an alibi, and how helpful she'd been in translating Parihaan's diary.

Then about how he'd suspected Nu and Nan Ji, but

their shoes and alibis had cleared them both. He spoke about how Geagle was a prime suspect, but was now instrumental in keeping Parihaan safe from the person with the knife.

"That's why you've had no sleep!" Mothy slapped his forehead.

"Partly. Also, nightmares. Now I'm trying to make sense of if it was Veluse or Captain Blutro that did this."

The night air was still warm from the heat the sun had left behind, but, as they walked around talking, it began to bite. A few passengers were passing around. Tinni and Tanni were spotting the stars as they appeared in the sky. Slavidus was teaching Yifi to steer the peaceful ship. Stra and Haatji were trading bags of spices and herbs for waking up in the morning. Froderyk and Dlumi were in a deep conversation about economics as they arm wrestled. Some of the crew were singing shanties to themselves in the crisp energy of the early evening.

"I saw the night Parihaan and Veluse fought. It was a week before you arrived. He showed us a painting he'd started of the Captain and he was getting really into the description of the Captain. Parihaan and her nasty friend, Chelsii, both laughed, but Parihaan also called out a slur about Veluse's romantic preferences. Oh boy did he ark up. It was like watching two dogs trying to bite each other.

After that they never spoke again except to make nasty comments back and forth. I think Veluse was quite isolated after that too, though. He has only just started to come back into his," Mothy waved his hands about in a theatrical fashion, "energy? It wasn't until Yifi made friends with him a few days before Plugh that he even looked at anyone else. I tried cheering him up but... well... when he's morose, he is a big black cloud."

"It's a bit juvenile, but I have seen people do that before. Quite often at festivals in Plugh. That gives him a clear motive though."

"May I throw a pin in your soup?"

"An odd expression, but I think I understand the meaning."

"Veluse is prone to sulking. Not aggravated violence." Mothy said. "Also, Captain Blutro rarely goes down to the hull for anything. It is possible that the shoe prints you saw were from a scuffle, but they could have also been from people just passing on the hull landing."

"I mean... it's possible."

"You've put a lot of effort into this idea so far, but I think you need to consider it could also have been an accident."

Wolflock ran his thumb nail in the zigzagging grooves of the shoe nail in his pocket.

"Mr Felen!"

Both boys looked up to see Captain Blutro stomping towards them. "Captain?"

"I told you to let this go! Did I not specify that there would be consequences if you didn't drop this damned business about-"

"Captain, I don't understand," Wolflock cut him off, frowning.

"The flour in the kitchen! Geagle just saw it and-"

"I'm sorry, Captain!" Mothy stepped between them, smiling sweetly, as he scratched his ear. "That was my fault. Wolflock and I were conducting an experiment and we needed to see if flour could be used to track the footprints of ghosts."

Captain Blutro and Wolflock stared at him.

"Oh. I see. Very well. I'm sorry to have accused you, Mr Felen. Mothy, go clean up the flour."

"Aye, aye, Captain!" Mothy saluted and charged off, giving Wolflock a wink behind the Captain's back.

"Again, my apologies. Good evening." He patted Wolflock's shoulder and moved to let Slavidus know to finish up his steering lesson so he could take over at the helm soon.

"It is likely to not be the last time. Merry part, Captain." He could help but smirk as the Captain walked away.

With his favourite company otherwise engaged and doubt shrouding his web of analysis, he thought speaking with Parihaan about his dilemma would provide him with some clarity. Most of the company on the top deck had retired to prepare for dinner.

He descended into the passenger hallway. As the crew did their daytime to night time changeover, someone would come and shake the fairy dust lanterns and brighten them up a bit. The eerie, nautical blue white glow and the slosh of the waves peeling away from the ship had become a great comfort to Wolflock these past few weeks. His stomach twisted as he wondered if Parihaan had felt the same comfort. He felt so torn, given her treatment of the company, his friends, and her beliefs.

As he laid his hand on her door he steeled himself. He'd have to have a stern conversation with her about this. He didn't like being conflicted in his motivations. Not one bit.

He opened his mouth to speak as he opened the door, only to see the hooded figure over Parihaan, holding a small pouch with their silver nails glinting in the light reflecting from the river. They turned to him in the darkness and gasped. The room reeked of a pungent odour, and the setting sun bouncing off the water gave the person a perfect silhouette, obscuring their appearance besides the hood and cloak. They threw a handful of herbs in Wolflock's face and tried to push past, but he lashed out, grabbing their left arm.

They hissed in pain and shoved him away, slipping from his grasp. The bright light had seared his eyes, as well as the sting from the herbs in them, and he could only see the imprint of the silhouette as he dashed into the hall. He blinked several times to clear his vision, but they were gone.

Growling, he wiped his face over and over on his sleeve, but the pungent herb just made his eyes water more until it was washed away by his tears. Anger bubbled up inside him and he glared back at Parihaan. She was in danger again and he had been the only person who could save her.

"Damn the Captain. If I have to tear this ship apart I won't let your justice go unserved."

CHAPTER 11

A Dance of Deception

Wolflock paced back and forth in Parihaan's room well past dinner, ignoring Nu when she popped in to give her patient her evening treatment. She asked about the herb on the blanket, but Wolflock grunted an unintelligible response and continued pacing. He wasn't sure how much time had passed, but Mothy came in with a cold dinner for him and a tray of tea.

"Are you troubled? You look troubled."

"Why now, though? Everyone was active and milling around. They could have been seen!"

"I'll take that as a yes. Did you discover something

new?" Mothy sat on the desk, picking at Wolflock's dinner.

"The silver is from nail polish paint. Or finger nails with paint on them. It makes sense now. It all makes sense and yet it doesn't! I have the pieces. I'm sure. The threads are right there. There are so many pieces. They nearly fit together, but then they are just not right. It's like wet puzzle pieces that are warped out of shape."

"Mmhmm." Mothy kept picking at the plate of vegetables and salted meat.

"I have the nail, the prints, the silver on the railing, the silver on the wall..."

"Silver on the walls would be expensive." Mothy scratched his chin as he added the comment mockingly.

"I have the blood under her nails which would be from a wound on someone's arm. It will be their dominant arm." Wolflock gripped his own and scratched at it incessantly. "Then I have the person with the strange, swirling, triple bladed knife. Parihaan's diary as well. All the pieces. Geagle's letters, your footprints, Nan Ji's shoes..."

"Oh, so you do know I'm here," Mothy chuckled and finished off a potato.

"Now I have this herb. By the gods it stinks."

"Herb? Wait. Show me," Mothy hopped off the desk and pinched it from Parihaan's blanket. "Oh gosh that's awful! And expensive."

"Expensive? How?" Wolflock stopped his pacing.

"This is dried ginkgo fruit and leaves. It smells like vomit. There's some in the hull. It's used for making you smarter."

Wolflock eyed Mothy with a raised eyebrow. "Have you been taking it?"

Mothy blushed. "No!" He reached for his face but pinned his hand back down to his side. "Oh fine, I have. Nu has been teaching me about some of her favourite herbs. They don't have the fruit though. Nu had a single one in her jewellery box to be a nasty surprise for thieves."

"Good to know. I wonder if Stra has any on board."

"He might, but, like I said, it's terribly expensive. The plants are hard to grow and are ancient. You can only get them in South Xiayah and some parts of Ulusai'il."

"You are a surprising wealth of knowledge today, my friend."

"What can I say? Every day is a new day, and I've barely seen you for three days."

Mothy clapped Wolflock on the shoulder, laughing, then pulled his hand away. "What's that? I didn't know Veluse had *silver paint.*" Mothy smirked and wiped some off of Wolflock's shoulder. "He was holding out the good stuff. My fish would have been amazing with this!"

Wolflock froze.

"Silver paint? What do you mean?"

"You've got a good smudge on your coat. It's quite pretty."

Wolflock stripped off his jacket and had a closer look. It was identical to the silver he'd seen on the wall, the railing and Parihaan's cheek. He could tell by the tiny flecks of glitter throughout it. It wasn't solid silver streaks or a single colour, but a varnish of multiple silvers.

His two main suspects had touched his shoulder today. That meant that the person who had pushed Parihaan down the stairs, the person who had crept into her room with the herbs just now, had touched Wolflock's shoulder.

But how could he get them to reveal themselves? He'd have to test them both and see who had silver nails. He picked at his own nails, wondering why he hadn't seen it on either of them earlier. As he picked his nails he scraped the dirt out from under his thumb.

"That's it!"

"Of course it is!" Mothy laughed. "What is?"

"The paint is under their nails! They have the silver paint under the nails. It was under their nails!"

"Under the nails? That's a weird place to paint nails, isn't it?"

"It is if you have strong nails, but some people paint the underside to add to the aesthetic, artistic flare, and strengthen their nails so they don't break as easily. Sometimes just working with paint will leave it under your nails too."

"So, you're leaning more to this being Veluse?"

"I'm not entirely sure yet, but it is definitely between him and the Captain."

"How are we going to find out who it is?"

"Well..." Wolflock began pacing again, grinning as the plan formulated before him, "We will need to do something that will get them to grip something soft to get the silver paint. It will have to be tonight, too."

"Why tonight?"

"Because, if we wait too long, the paint will be dry and we are lucky that they've got the silver paint on their nails again. It's something they didn't realise was a clue."

"It will have to be something that everyone is drawn to so they let their guard down."

"Like a dance!"

Wolflock squinted as he thought. "Yes. But not just any dance. It has to be something they'd feel obligated to come to."

"Hmm.... what kind of dance would Veluse and the Captain feel like they needed to come to?"

"Well, Veluse would come for the artistic nature, but he'd feel obligated to come if he had a part in it. Aha! I've got it!" Wolflock snapped his fingers, "Tell him that he was the inspiration for the dance as his words helped me choreograph it from my designs. He saw me drawing the shoe prints and commented on them, so if we remind him of that he'll be there."

"And what about the Captain? He's started his shift at the helm. This is very short notice, you realise?" Mothy crossed his legs and pondered their plan. "What if I told everyone it was my birthday?"

"Is it?"

"No."

"Then don't do that. We need it to be a bit more believable. If we keep it close to the truth then the celebration and dancing will feel more real."

They sat and stood in silence for a long time as they thought.

"Real..." Wolflock hummed. "That's it! Slavidus!"

"No. Mothy." His friend put his hand to his chest.

"Not that! Slavidus! We need to get him to give the pendant to Yifi in public and then we'll all have something to celebrate."

"Gosh, Lockie. Isn't that a bit too invasive?"

"He's been needing to do it for days now." Wolflock

waved his objection away. "This is just giving him a helping hand."

"I'm in. What's the plan?"

Wolflock explained his idea, and after a quick search of Slavidus' room for the enchanted necklace, they concluded it was still in his pocket. They found Slavidus and Yifi on the deck deep in conversation as they leaned on the railing of the portside mid deck.

"Are you sure you want to do it? I have more practice." Mothy nudged him as they loitered around the centre mast.

"Everyone on the ship is swayed more easily by your suggestions. They'll all come up here if you ask them to. They'll suspect something if I ask them."

"I mean... you're not wrong."

"I rarely am. Now go and make sure they have an audience or Slavidus might blow off the ruse."

Mothy rolled his eyes and headed off to start spreading the word that Slavidus was about to do something amazing. Wolflock flicked a rag over the lantern illuminating the area behind Slavidus and Yifi. They didn't pay him much heed, exactly as he'd hoped.

The crew and company began gathering on the deck, watching for this "special" thing Mothy had warned them of. From the shadows Wolflock could see everyone who had passed by, keeping a close eye on anyone going back down the stairs. It was Mothy's job to keep them up here by any means necessary.

Wolflock knew the crew's schedule and during the night shift on the weekday Sollempus, the only crew working would be Kolor on watch, the Captain on the helm, Hognut and Goden on deck duties.

As everyone milled curiously around the deck, he seized the moment. Wolflock held the dimmed fairy dust lantern in his left hand, kept his shoulders tight, chin down, and his right hand ready. It wasn't his dominant hand, so he stretched his fingers as if he was preparing for playing a concert on the violin. With confident strides, he walked behind them, bumping his whole arm into Slavidus. In one smooth movement he plunged his fingers into Slavidus pocket and yanked out the chain the huge citrine pendant was attached to.

"Sorry!" Wolflock raised his hands, flinging the pendant across the floor. "Sorry! I wasn't looking where I was going."

"Be more careful, Mr Felen," Slavidus scolded. As he looked to the clattering sound across the deck his eyes went wide.

Wolflock looked to the noise as if he didn't know what it was and shook the lantern, illuminating their section of the deck in a beautiful blue and white light. Everyone on the deck had turned their attention to the display.

Slavidus dived forward and clasped the necklace with both hands, kneeling on the ground with an expression as if he had been struck by lightning. Without looking at anyone he stood up and moved his hand back to his pocket.

Wolflock felt a pang of fear. He'd put this together so strategically. Slavidus couldn't back out now. He would ruin everything.

"Yifi, what does he have there?" Wolflock murmured to her, nudging her with his elbow.

Yifi shrugged, tilting her head to the side. "Slavidus? That looked very shiny. What is it?"

The tall man swallowed, his face white. "Uh... It's... something I've been saving... for you?"

Yifi raised her elegant brown eyebrow. "Oh? You didn't need to get me anything."

"I know. I just..." he looked around to see the sparkling eyes of the curious crowd and shrank. "I just didn't know how to give it to you."

He held out his hand with the large citrine pendant with elegant copper filigree. It looked large, but not magical.

"I... umm... bought this at the Krieger Zwerg market

and it allows you to be perceived however you want to be perceived. I thought... since you're cursed... well..."

Yifi gasped. "Slavidus..."

"Would you like this? Have I overstepped a boundary? You don't have to take it if you don't want-"

Yifi threw her arms around his neck and laid a passionate kiss on his lips.

"I don't know if it even works," Slavidus pleaded.

"Put it on her, then!" Mothy called from the back of the crowd.

Laughter tittered through the crowd and Yifi lifted her hair for Slavidus to fasten the necklace around her neck. The moment it was latched tiny translucent orange sparkles began to appear above Yifi's head and float down onto her body. As each twinkle touched her, it sent out a small glowing ripple about the size of her palm. To the rest of the crew and company it looked like Yifi was shrouded in a layer of disturbed water. After a few moments the ripples settled and Yifi as she wished to be perceived stood before them.

The changes were subtle, but effective. Her face was more square, her hair less lustrous. For the first time Wolflock could see pores in her skin and fine hairs on her face. Her eyebrows looked thicker and more natural, and she looked overall more average. The thing that stood out the most though, was her smile. Instead of her usual restrained, closed mouth smile, Yifi had a grin that lit up her entire face, lifting her rosy cheeks and squinting her eyes.

Slavidus stood in awe of the transformation. After a few moments he cupped her cheek in his hand and smiled adoringly back at her. "I guess the necklace is broken, because I don't see any change at all besides that you look happier."

They kissed again and the audience on the deck broke out into raucous applause. As Wolflock looked around for Veluse and the Captain, he couldn't help but notice that the people around him looked happier than they had in a long while. Had this been something they'd needed but didn't realise?

He moved away as some of the people moved forward to start asking Yifi and Slavidus all manner of probing questions in their excitement. He walked up the stairs to Captain Blutro, grinned smugly as Mothy called for a dance to begin. Haatji, Stra, Nan Ji and Kolor lingered along the edges, choosing to not partake in the revelry, but instead clap and sing along.

"Are you trying to get rid of my first mate?" Captain Blutro chuckled.

"I have no idea what you could be referring to."

"He did need a bit of a push, though, didn't he?"

"Oh he was going to linger on that until they had well and truly parted, I have no doubt. He's not born under the Nymph sign, is he?"

"How did you guess?"

"My sister always said that Nymph people were fickle and indecisive. I wonder if there is more stock in that than I previously gave it credit for."

"You're an odd chap, Wolflock. Thoughtful. But odd. I'd say you would be born under Golem or Griffin."

A glint of inspiration flashed across his mind. "Myna said you can tell someone's sign by shaking their hand. Care to have a more informed guess?"

Captain Blutro held out his rough hand and Wolflock took it with both, giving them a firm squeeze, pressing the Captain's fingertips into the back of his hand.

"Definitely Centaur. A Golem shake is less confident."

"I see." Wolflock hummed, looking at the back of his hand. Nothing.

"Well, am I right?"

Wolflock gave his head a little shake, bringing himself back to the conversation. "I'm born in Yulae Nibit'solos, under Chimera."

"Ah! Of course! That makes more sense. Did you

know the Quaretz twins will be doing readings for everyone after we get through the mountain pass?"

"Truly? That will be fascinating. If you'll excuse me, Captain. I have mischief calling my name."

"What will I do with you, Mr Felen?" the Captain groaned as Wolflock laughed down the stairs to join the dancing.

The group had joined in a large circle that was making fun, rippling patterns. One by one the people would run into the centre of the circle, still gripping their neighbours. They would kick into the middle and step back out, singing a merry chorus of nonsense.

Mothy caught his eye and nodded to his left. Wolflock followed his line of sight and spotted Veluse between Yifi and Tinni. The tiny little girl was tiptoeing her way through the dance, occasionally being hoisted into the air by Veluse and her mother with delighted squeals.

Wolflock waited for them to come around and pushed his way in with a shake of Veluse's shoulder. The artist smiled broadly, his wavy auburn hair bouncing around his smooth face, as he let Wolflock between him and the child.

They ran into the middle and out again, holding their neighbours hands and arms, trusting the support they were offered. Wolflock laughed along with them from the heart, but he made sure he changed his grip often with Veluse.

Finally, the song, chant, dancing and stomping came to a close, giving Wolflock a chance to check his hand and arm. Nothing. Had he taken too long? Was the paint already dry? Had he been mistaken.

With a false smile he made his way to Mothy.

"I want to observe them once more. We didn't get it. Can you get them to dance again?"

"Can a fish swim? Merry meet, everyone! Let's celebrate just once more! One for Miss Yifi, and one for Slavidus!"

The applause raised again and Wolflock's eyes darted around. There was an odd illumination to their hands due to the angle the fairy dust lantern he had on his hip. The light was shining up through some of the people nearest him. A few of the other lanterns had been placed on seats and crates so people could dance in the brightness too.

Then he saw it. The glint of silver on the underside of a set of perfectly repainted nails just next to him.

Painted nails on the smooth jewelled hands of Haatji.

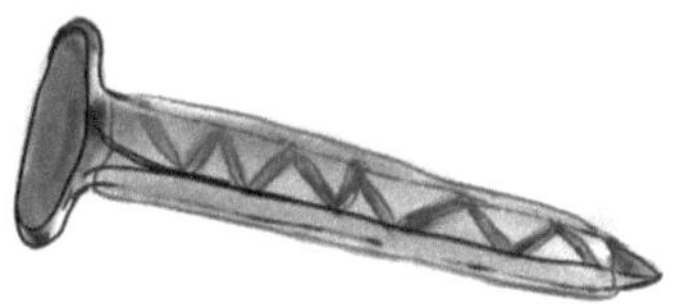

CHAPTER 12

The Nail and the Lady

Mothy started up a new dance with clapping, crossing, back slapping hands, twirling and changing partners. Tanni caught Wolflock and pulled him over to be her dance partner for the first set.

Clap, clap, cross, clap, slap, cross, twirl and grab.

Grogen raced downstairs to grab his guitar. He re-emerged moments late and played a plucky ditty on it. Wolflock moved to Froderyk as a dance partner after the twirl.

Clap, clap, cross, clap, slap, cross, twirl and grab.

His eyes were locked on Haatji. She had the silver paint. She had slapped Parihaan. But she had an alibi. The twins Faleen and Bleen had told him that during the time of the accident she had been with them. How had he not realised the curled toed shoes were hers?

The last three days flashed through his mind. He'd seen her wearing them the night Parihaan fought with everyone on the deck. She had still been wearing them when Parihaan was brought up from the hull. She didn't have scratches on her arm.

Not on her right arm...

Haatji sat on a small box clapping to the tune and singing along, but when Tinni danced with Grogen and he put her on his shoulders, Haatji pointed with her left hand.

It was all coming together. The shoes, the silver, the scratches. Haatji had been in Parihaan's room earlier with the herbs.

Why had she helped him translate the diary, though? He felt like such a fool. He had to tell her he knew. He had to confront her.

Clap, clap, cross, clap, slap, cross, twirl and grab.

"Why do you have your 'my web of ideas isn't making sense' face," Mothy caught hold of him and began the clapping dance.

"Because it isn't," Wolflock muttered. "Veluse and Captain Blutro don't have the nail polish on."

"Thank their lucky stars then, ay?"

As they twirled, Wolflock wanted to cry out in triumph. "Stars! Mothy! That's it! Stars!"

"You're doing that thing again-"

He started to laugh at Wolflock, but they were both caught by new partners.

Clap, clap, cross, clap, slap, cross, twirl and grab.

He danced with Dlumi and moved closer and closer to Haatji. With the high energy of the room, he was certain his next action would go unnoticed by the larger crowd.

Clap, clap, cross, clap, slap, cross, twirl.

Wolflock twirled and grabbed Haatji's arm, trying to pull her into the dance. She winced as his hand closed tightly around her left forearm, and her golden eyes were aflame with shock.

"Wolflock!"

"Come on, Haatji! Everyone is having so much fun!" He tugged harder.

"I said no!"

A clap mingled with all the others as she struck his cheek. The sting shocked him, but the breeze told him where the silver had been left behind.

"What has gotten into you!?" Haatji gasped, clutching her left arm to her chest.

"Did you realise Parihaan had the same marks on her cheek and at the scene where she was pushed down the stairs?"

"I-I don't know what you are talking about."

"I found your shoes as well. The exact same print that was on the hull landing, fresh in the dust alongside Parihaan's."

Haatji recoiled, unable to meet his eye.

"Why did you try to frame Mothy when you found out I was on the case? He has been kind and thoughtful to everyone on board."

"I did not do that," she whimpered. "You cannot prove it."

"You had the twins tell me you were with them when Parihaan fell, but they were on the deck watching the stars with the children before they came to give you a reading. You lied to me. You only joined them after you pushed her down the stairs."

She didn't speak.

"Show me your dominant hand. Show me your left hand."

She turned it over. She didn't even need to pull up the sleeve for him to see the deep scratches all the way down to her thumb.

As Haatji's eyes filled with defeated tears, Wolflock felt crushed. This wasn't the happy result, the 'ahah' moment he'd hoped for. It felt terrible.

"It was an accident," she sobbed.

Frightened for her modesty and drawing a scene, he jerked his head to the cabins. She was smaller than him, and he had no fear she could push him to his end down another set of stairs. They walked down the stairs together, but out of habit, Wolflock moved to Parihaan's room.

"Tell me what happened."

Haatji sat down at the desk chair while Wolflock leaned on the empty bedside table.

"After I left the kitchen I went back to my room, but, before I could go inside, I saw Parihaan heading downstairs. I knew she was looking for more drinking alcohol and I had to stop her. She had brought the women in our country to terrible disrepute and I needed to stop her from doing it anymore."

"That does not work in your favour, Haatji."

"I know. I know. I just... I was just going to drag her back upstairs. When I reached her on the landing in the hull, she was wobbling. I tried to take the lantern from her, but she held it tight. We argued. I can barely even remember what I said. I just know it was stupid."

Haatji couldn't raise her eyes to meet him.

"She pushed me against the railing. I thought I was going to fall over it. I pushed her back against the wall and knocked the lantern from her hand down the stairs. We pushed away from each other and I moved to the stairs going up. I was done. I didn't want to fight her anymore. I knew I would never get through to her. She had made me so mad and I didn't have the energy for her anymore. She..."

Haatji looked up finally and touched her face as if it were a sculpture of sand and would crumble under anything but the lightest touch.

"She called me a *libiwat alturab.* It means 'lioness of dirt'."

"Why is that offensive?" Wolflock queried, thinking he had been called much worse by his peers in Plugh.

"In a land like Uluken where water is a precious resource, it is hard to wash dirt from everything, so we look after our possessions and homes with a different kind of respect than some of the other nations. Lioness, I've learned outside of Uluken, are thought of as regal, powerful creatures. For us that live with them, they are frightening and are considered," she shuffled her shoulders uncomfortably, "promiscuous."

"Again, your family aren't Trostons. That sort of thing isn't such a terrible insult, is it? It's more of a value judgement on the person using the terms."

Haatji picked at her nails, silver paint smudging on the orange top coat "to most, no. It is a terribly light insult that isn't worth a backwards glance over your shoulder."

"Then why did it bother you so much?"

"It... It will not make sense without a very long tale. I'm sure you don't want to-"

"It's not like we won't have time. You know about her past, I suppose it's only fair she gets to hear yours," Wolflock shrugged and gestured to the sleeping Parihaan.

Haatji shuffled in her seat as if she was about to leave, but then relaxed back into it with a sigh.

"I am the eldest daughter of the Semiramis family. We are an ancient line and it is my duty to set the example my younger sisters are to follow. I was courted and married to a man with wealth and stature. He is a powerful merchant of spices and fine fabrics in Uluken. We married while I was quite young and things were good for several years. The more I helped to increase trade with outside nations, though, the more possessive and jealous he became. One day he grew so mad that he threw me through a stained glass window."

Haatji pinched the edges of the veil covering her face and drew it away, revealing deep jagged scars all over her nose, lips, chin and cheeks. One of her lips was so torn that it hooked into the deep set scar running to her ear. The disfigurement of her lips and her missing front teeth caused her lisp.

"After that time he grew a wicked liking to beating me. Never as badly as the first time, but more hands on. I lost many teeth because of this. I began wearing the burqa and niqab to hide my broken face and the shame that I stayed with him. I was frightened I would damage my family's honour. I believed I would be destitute. I had no idea what to do, and I was so unaware of how he isolated me from my friends and family. He kept me locked up in our manor and made sure that my only friends were the transient people coming to make trade deals. But all of them would leave. When we had guests, he would return to being a perfect gentleman to me and I thought maybe this time he would go back to his old happy self. I was always wrong."

Wolflock squirmed. He knew these sorts of things went on, but he'd never seen the magnitude of damage they could do to someone. Haatji would have been unrecognisable to her original appearance.

"One day we had travellers coming from Shiriling and I tended to them as always, organising the lighter deals and enjoying the reprieve from pain. I met a man, though. He was so thoughtful. He was so kind. He was enchanted by me and we spoke for hours and hours. He even told me that he would delay the trading deals deliberately to spend more time with me. He saw my face by accident and wanted to know how he could help. I got him to send a letter to my parents telling them everything. I had thought for a long time that my husband had been destroying my letters, no matter how innocent they were. I fell in love with the heart of that man. Yekrid Ollilliam. When he left, I suffered a sadness and a longing I'd never experienced before."

She sighed and fixed her veil over her face once more.

"I waited a month and started to think he had deceived me, but my parents came with all of my cousins and nephews. They broke me free from my prison, but, even though I was safe for a while, my husband was powerful. When I filed for divorce, he had contacts in the administration offices lose them each time. He was getting a lot of power from the use of my family's name and he wasn't about to give it up. We had been married seven years and he would have been ashamed that I had born no children with him, either. I was grateful."

Wolflock was engrossed in the story, but, when Haatji paused, Parihaan let out a low moan. They both jumped and waited, but her normal breathing returned.

"I publicly disowned him, but then he started sending assassins after me. Whenever we caught them, their contract was to 'end the lioness'." Her nose wrinkled into a snarl as she spoke. "All I could think of was, 'how dare he'. But my parents knew what to do. For my safety and the safety of our family, I had to leave for some time. They would become good friends with my husband's associates to force the social pressure on him to be civil. They also reported his behaviour to the Guard and had him bogged down with mediation and behavioural lessons. I decided to travel and see if I could find the Shiriling trader who saved me, but my husband had assassins stationed at the Northern pass, so I had to travel all the way through Grothener to the Zilber River and then North from here."

"So, being called a 'dirt lioness' triggered those terrible memories and anxieties in you?" he confirmed, grasping the story with keen interest.

"Yes. I charged back down the stairs at her and slapped her face. I knew I shouldn't, but I felt as if the rage inside me had taken control. I stepped back, shocked at myself. She stepped back, too, but it put her off balance on the top of the stairs. She waved her arms around, but couldn't get her balance. I saw what was happening, so I ran forward and caught her arm, but she was too heavy. She dragged her nails down my left arm and slipped from my grasp."

Wolflock frowned as the scene played vividly

through his mind. "Why didn't you call for help?"

"I did not think anyone would believe me. I... I think I am used to people having to accept someone else's word over mine. Everyone had seen us fight earlier and I just did not think that, if I came forward, I would be listened to. I also thought she was dead. There was nothing I could do as penance for a dead woman."

"There is for a living one, though." Wolflock thought about each of his threads and how they still weren't linked to Haatji, yet. "Your shoes. You threw them out of Mothy's window. You did that after you went through my room, yes? You saw the design of your shoe print and realised I was catching on to you."

"I did look through your room first. I saw the shoe print and some of the details you'd written down and I wasn't sure if you thought it was me and was just playing with me. I had enjoyed talking to you and, before I saw your notebook, I thought we were becoming good acquaintances. I was hurt to think you were only talking to me because you suspected my involvement. When I found your notebook I ran back into my room, found the shoes and didn't know what to do. I knew you would be out soon and walked to the stairs, thinking I'd just throw them off the side, but then I realised everyone would see. So, I rushed into your room but the window wouldn't open. I just automatically went into Mothy's room next and threw them out. You were coming down the hall as I came out of Mothy's room, but you were so deep in thought you didn't see."

"I see. And the herbs? The pungent ones? Mothy said they're for waking someone out of unconsciousness. You got them from Stra didn't you? I saw you in the dining hall talking to him. You were trying to wake her up. Why?" He put his index knuckle to his bottom lip.

Haatji nodded, "I spoke with Stra and got something he recommended. Nan Ji is so strict with the herbs and the reasons he sells them, plus his daughter would hear and she is good friends with you both. Stra had them for sale and helped me get a good potency, but you interrupted me before I could use them properly. I was just trying to fix what I'd done. I thought, if I could wake her up, then maybe I could make amends."

"Mothy said they wouldn't work. People are unconscious for a reason and, sometimes, the sleep will help them heal better than being awake." She ran her fingers tips around the scratch on her hand.

"And, what about the knife?"

Haatji blinked, "What knife?"

"The night Parihaan fell down the stairs I couldn't sleep, so I came in here to find someone standing over her with a three edged swirling knife."

"I have never heard of such a thing. The only time I came in here was with the herbs to make up for the accident."

Accident...

The word bounced around in Wolflock's head. In time with the echoing word he ran his thumbnail along the zig zagging groove of the shoe nail in his pocket.

"Tell me. When Parihaan slipped from your grasp did she fall right away?"

"No. She teetered on the top step. I had slipped and fallen onto the first set of stairs. I remember seeing her with one leg in the air and one heel caught on the top step. I jumped up to grab her flailing arms, but I was too late..." Haatji's eyes welled with tears and she shook with sobs. "I prayed every night since."

She did. Wolflock knew she did. He heard her through the window the night he'd seen the person with the knife. Did that mean someone else on board wanted Parihaan dead?

He drew out the nail and looked over it. If Parihaan had been shoved from the events Haatji described, the nail would have a single long scrape down it. But she had teetered leaving the distinct zig zag marking he'd been holding these past few days.

"I know it was an accident." he whispered to himself. "I knew it was an accident!"

"H-how?" Haatji hiccupped.

"See the pattern on this nail? It came from Parihaan's shoe. The pattern of the leather shows that it was slowly wriggled free from the shoe, not wrenched out."

"That is not very much evidence, Wolflock." She smiled sadly. "Not enough to prove my innocence to the Captain. Are you going to turn me in?"

It was his turn to decide. He owed them both that. Parihaan deserved justice, but what justice could be truly given when this was a terrible accident? A scandal willed with lies and secrets, but the only person who was acting with any kind of malice was the victim and the mysterious knife person.

"No. I won't. But we need your help. I don't know why, but Parihaan is in danger. Nu, Geagle and I take turns watching her room and keeping her safe. If you really want to make recompense for being part of her accident, you need to help care for her until she wakes up."

"That is something I can do, and will do happily." Her shoulders relaxed and she smiled at Parihaan.

"Fantastic. Maybe then I can get some sleep and you can cover my shifts."

"You are an odd person, Mr Felen. Odd. But good.

I'm not sure I have the words in a language you would understand. In my language it is *Easifa*."

"What does that mean?" Wolflock asked with his head cocked to the side.

"Firestorm."

"Firestorm? Why is that?" It didn't sound like a particularly good title to have.

"In Uluken there are crops that grow and grow in the desert but only put out their seeds when they go through fire. The easifa wipes everything out to black dust, and reduces it all to only the strongest bones. After this happens, the seeds all spring forth from the ground and flourish. If you are not careful it will catch onto the storage sheds or houses though. The easifa also strikes at random. Sometimes it will not come for years. Sometimes it comes in half a year. The easifa wields tremendous power recklessly, destroying everything in its path. But, then, the fruits of your labour are revealed with new growth and understanding. You, Mr Felen, are an easifa."

During Haatji's explanation, she had sat herself back upright and regained her regal aura. She looked through Parihaan's cosmetics and knelt beside her to smooth a creamy lotion on her skin and oil her hair.

"She is blessed with such thick hair. It is a sign of strong health."

"I am sure she will recover." Wolflock nodded.

Now that he'd solved the mystery and gotten the answers, he expected her to open her eyes in a daze and ask where she was and what happened. Nothing. She stayed silent. But he'd finished the case. He had the answers. She had to wake up. Perhaps he would just have to wait a few more minutes. Haatji's touch would certainly make her stir.

Nothing. Silence.

He frowned. "I have a message to give her. I... When will she wake up, Haatji?"

Haatji turned to look at him curiously. "Wolflock, she may never wake up. When she does wake up, she may never walk or move again. That is what I heard Nan Ji telling Stra. What message did you have for her?"

"But I worked so hard to keep her safe and Nu has been working so diligently on healing her. Why wouldn't she wake up?"

Haatji sighed. "Sometimes, it's not enough, my friend. You have to know that within yourself you have done the right thing, regardless of what the outcome may be. Acting with integrity leads to a more peaceful mind. Helping Parihaan as we make our way to Creast will help me, also. I will do my duty and keep her safe and well in all the capacity I can."

He pouted, crossing his arms, dissatisfied with that answer. "But I have a message for her."

Haatji chuckled and rose from her knees. "She may be able to hear you. Perhaps you need to tell her the message as often as you can to make sure she can hear it."

"That's a lot of effort."

"Doing the right thing often is. It is a relief to know a better way to accomplish it, though. I was so frightened for her these past few days."

She moved away and allowed him the space next to Parihaan. Haatji packed up the cosmetics and oils as he thought about what he was going to say.

"You thought you didn't have friends. I did too. I mean. I thought I didn't have friends. For a long time, actually. You thought people didn't care and that they thought you were weird or not good enough. So, you did things that weren't good for you to give yourself the feeling of being loved. You drank alcohol. Grogen used to smoke. Yifi used to drink a magic brew. Hognut still smokes."

He touched her hand. "It can be really hard to talk about how you're hurting and sometimes you really need someone to make space for you to talk about it and not feel like you're going to be shunned or kicked out of home. Grogen said it takes a village giving you unconditional love to help you heal. I think it also takes the choice to want to heal. Grogen, Yifi, Froderyk and Fuhji were all prepared to be your village. Now you have Haatji, Nu, Geagle, Mothy and I too."

He felt his chest ache. He had just wished someone had said this to him while he was at Plugh. Even if he rebuffed it out of pride or ignored them out of shame. He just wished someone had told him...

"You have friends and we're going to look after you."

He stood up and wiped his eyes on his sleeve, glaring down at Parihaan for making him upset. "So, you'd best get better faster, because I need someone new to play chess with."

He nodded quickly to Haatji and strode out of the room and up to the top deck, hiding in the shadows. Wolflock looked back to the group of revellers still dancing and clapping on the deck. Geagle had taken up a drum and Hognut had found a second guitar, and they played merrily along together.

He stood back and watched, processing everything he'd learned and everything he'd been through since the Krieger Zwerg dock. It had been one of the most intense weeks of his life. He snuck some fruit out of the kitchen and hid away in his room eating it, enjoying his solitude. As he drifted off to sleep with a half eaten apple, he had to admit that it had been, at least, a very trying few days.

The ship sailed on through the evening and when everyone awoke and rose for breakfast, they saw the mountains were moving further and further away from the sides of the Silver Hair. They were finally coming into Hatfjorn Lake.

"Lockie!" Mothy ran up to him in his pyjamas and dragged him to the port side of the ship. "Look out there!"

Wolflock rubbed his sleepy eyes and looked across the crystal clear blue water. The water seemed to be breaking in odd patterns and small black fins rose and sank like a turning wheel.

"What is it?"

"Dolphins!"

The crew and company heard him and ran to the side to see.

"There's one! I see it!" Tinni cried out, her mother catching her before she tipped over the taffrail.

"And there! Another!"

"They're coming closer!"

Dolphins started to circle the ship and leap out, chasing the waves that spread from the sides. Underneath seemed to be a streak of silver and grey that would vanish when they tried to determine what they were.

For a few minutes everyone laughed and smiled, watching the wild lake creatures flit around the ship like butterflies around flowers. Some even started doing somersaults and swimming on their sides to wave their fins. The joy that their mere presence brought was overwhelmingly healing to them all.

After the dolphins had departed and the guests went to breakfast, Grogen regaled them with stories of dolphins saving the crew from drowning and freezing to death, as well as the mythology of how they were such a good omen.

The next week passed quickly. Between alternating shifts with those looking after Parihaan and getting into slightly less mischief than usual, Wolflock found himself entertained. Every day they looked for movement in the unconscious woman, but nothing could be seen. Just as he began growing bored of the routine, the crew began acting as if they were in the know about something special. After being given the heads up by the Captain that they ought to get a good view after breakfast, Wolflock and Mothy snuck into the crows nest. The Silver Ice Hair came into the view of the deep blue waters meeting the pale horizon. Everywhere before them was a pristine sheet of glassy water.

Wolflock and Mothy looked out over the stern of the ship and enjoyed the wind catching their hair, trying to spot more dolphins. A sensation of pure ease washed over the ship. The magic of the River God Houl had transformed into the Goddess Hatfjorn of the inland sea.

"It's so calm..." Wolflock sighed.

Mothy chuckled, "It certainly is now that you've solved another mystery."

"I've been thinking of something all week. I want you to remind me of something when we get to Mystentine," Wolflock exhaled as he ran his thumb over the zigzagging pattern on the shoe nail in his pocket.

"What?"

"I need to find the best cobbler in Mystentine."

Pertmpus der 18th an Eulas Resari

Dirt MYna,

Lanke fa fumf fane lather. Orkowhl J ban bittet zu
her Barta hab ann nauan spieltirt. J fa nicht sarge
uf ther iz bese am mich is nicht. Ts iz sen nicht
bedeutung zu mich und J hafe fa ubertragan dat zu
tharn. Jnsbesandere seuread ther tun nicht schrab zu
mich tharmolber.

J sermift Drennan mehr als J rannen zage, aber ann
schipp iz nicht plaatz-ter fumf ann pferd. Bitte
mitteilen tharn uber mich abenteure zu enflaten
tharn herzansfummer. J ban bittet fa sins
sicherfreutet felagtertet tharn gartung. Ss lehr ss is
aufsemt fa unterhault J ban stellan fa garde nehman
gut pflege sen tharn.
J sremt fa garde ringen sinzu gesluthenaft scheler
is spätern. J hafe ser gefuhl is befuente und
sicherhat zu ser herrgele satenicht garben fa sinzu
andere Uissrita Thsen. J auch mecht is ann Zeit zu
untersuch sich zu aufsem regierung bannte ann
prufen. J garde ss ser par ann ger bannte austricken
fa und aufsem fa austricht sen ser seruppe sen
schsicher und suttenzeit.
J garde anerten ann tail mehr sertrauen ann mich
fähigkeite zu erhalten mich sitzen uzsai sersteunbet
ann zunkuft lather. J hafe nicht einet nur nach zu
hafet zu ahen haummerherz. Uber fa sins fehlerfrei

ein glaubet J habe haben sele beschäftigen zum der
abentete af der schipp.
J wurde schreib mehr aber der Kapitän hat fragt mich
zu frühstück.
Dine selschaftinger bruther.

Wolflück F. Felen

R.S. Mothy hat fragt zu schreib zu hi. J hab erzählt
them J wurde frag. Ze hlee iz mich nacherfullet
mich pflicht as ein freund. J erwart hi zu
nachlehnen them beurbach J kennt hi wurde par
sagen them zu spien an mich.
R.R.S. Uf J finde hi habe schreib zu them ein
versteckt. J wurde hennach mittelen hi as J gesehret
hine versneit uhrmuschel. Erinnern? Der einene hat
herrhein ein der karawane bezauberte fumf hi.

About the Author

Rhiannon is the walker between worlds. One foot in Earth, the other constantly stepping into Pelaia. As if gazing into a crystal ball, she sees this other world and all that happens within it with the clarity of someone staring through a veil. It is her purpose in life to transcribe these histories, adventures and mysteries for you to enjoy.

This witchy woman was raised by a fairy who taught her that there are all kinds of magic throughout the world. She taught Rhiannon to withhold judgement because you never truly know another's story. She also taught her that everyone, no matter how flawed, has something to give.

The adventures of Rhiannon's youth lead her through trials and dangers that taught her about the darkness within the world, but it also showed her that anything could be overcome. There was always a way. Surrounded by so much apathy and hopelessness, Rhiannon made it her goal in life to show others the light and that if they could dream it, they could do it.

The way she was shown this was through stories.

Stories of friendship, love, adventure, discovery, compassion, understanding, and kindness. All of these stories gave her new friends, new lessons, new life.

In the depths of her darkest place during year 11 and 12, when she felt at her loneliest, drugs surrounded her life in terrible ways, the self-worth of those she loved and admired crumbled, she was relentlessly bullied and felt friendless in her most trying years, she lived in squalor due to bureaucratic errors, and yet she still had to be "perfect". She had to perfectly excel in school, she had to perfectly remain calm and gentle in the face of abusive men, she had to be a perfect role model for all those around her. That craving for perfection in order to get love nearly killed her several times. In all of this darkness with politicians sacrificing real people and real environments for imaginary money, with teachers displaying no compassion for their students, with men abusing women and children, with communities vilifying those who needed them most, with injustice reigning and all hope seemingly lost... Puinteyle was born.

All of these pains in life were fixed in Puinteyle.

All of them were able to be mended and healed because of a conscientious effort. The people of Puinteyle wanted to be better than their problems. Puinteyle was where people made an effort to love freely and always sought to help each other, animals and the environment. Harmony. True and beautiful harmony. Where the pendulum never swayed too far away from that beautiful harmonious and happy point of balance.

But like in our lives, there is always obstacles to overcome and darkness to understand. Therefore, Puinteyle would always have its own inner turmoils to learn and grow from too. Thus, the stories never truly end.

Rhiannon has always lived and breathed stories, knowing her role in life is to be this guide through a new world for others. Her dream is to support her community with her stories, as well as creating a company where other artists can come together in celebration of Pelaia and all it has to offer.

Get More of the Magic & Mystery…

subscribe.rhiannoneltonauthor.com/more

If you want more clues, more magic and more mystery, let me know by going to the Case of the Bitter Draught subscribe page.

You'll get clues, maps, sketches, behind the scenes stories, lore and much more! You'll also be the first to know when a new story is coming out so you can solve the mystery before your friends.

If you sign up with the magical link below, you'll also get a free downloadable map to follow Wolflock's journey to Mystentine University.

subscribe.rhiannoneltonauthor.com/more

If you enjoyed this book, please leave a positive review online (where you purchased the book or on Goodreads), recommend this book to your friends or family, or purchase another copy to gift to a loved one.

Stay tuned for the next mystery in the series:

THE WOLFLOCK CASES

BOOK 6

THE CASE OF THE LOST MERMAID

www.rhiannoneltonauthor.com

 RhiDElton

 RhiannonEltonAuthor

 RhiDElton

 rhiannoneltonauthor

 Rhiannon D. Elton

 RhiDElton

THE WOLFLOCK CASES